The nation's press reports on the first edition of Power Calling—A Fresh Approach To Cold Calls & Prospecting:

"If telephone selling is an art in and of itself, Joan Guiducci could probably paint the Sistine Chapel with her receiver. Her book holds hundreds of ideas for sales professionals and the margins are lined with even more golden nuggets."
— *Personal Selling Power*

"*Power Calling* may be just the book for your business. Joan's creative approach is rich in examples and full of how-tos for the experienced and novice caller."
—*Profit,* an IBM magazine

"Joan has the right mixture of charm and sales push. She offers excellent training in a skill that daily becomes more essential: career survival by telephone."
— Joyce Lain Kennedy, Career advice columnist

"I read *Power Calling* without an iota of boredom. The book is void of lifeless theories and statistics. If you make cold calls on a regular basis, pick up this book."
— *Teleprofessional*

"*Power Calling* is a comprehensive guide to making calls that mean business. Cold calling can be difficult and uncomfortable, but it's also a good way to attract customers. With Guiducci's tips, the process becomes easier and even enjoyable." — *Entrepreneur*

Power Calling® II

How To Build New Business In A Crowded Marketplace
Copyright © 1995
Power Calling is a registered trademark of Tonino.
All rights reserved.

Editorial director
Kristen Muller Levine
San Francisco, CA

Graphics
Amy Hazel
Paris, France

ISBN 1–881833–01–1

Printed in the United States of America.

In memory of my Aunt Ruth

When you cannot see what is happening, do not stare harder. Relax and look gently with your inner eye.

—John Heider
The Tao of Leadership

Table of Contents

Acknowledgements   To my husband, Gino, who was always there. And to my editor, Kristen, who has an extraordinary vision for the written word and with whom I had the joy of collaborating. Many thanks to my designer, Amy, for making Power Calling look great. My sincere and deepest appreciation goes to family (Denise, Nelia, and Richard), Mark Lammers, and Dan Byrne for their encouragement and suggestions. Thanks to you all.

Joan Guiducci

Introduction

Welcome to Power Calling II. The suggestions found in this book are drawn from challenges salespeople have presented to me and from my own experience as a salesperson.

Power Calling is about building new business. In this program we discuss how the first call into an account remains a necessary, integral part of closing a sale. I have divided this book into 12 chapters, each covering an essential component. If you use them, these 12 components will change your mind on the importance and power of the finding your ideal accounts.

Aristotle said humans spend most of their life, planning their life. Yet it's baffling how so few of us take our planning out on the road for a spin. Together we'll organize a prospecting strategy—a plan for making new business contacts. The best way to develop Power Calling concepts is using an Action Planner—the 48-page companion guide to this book.

In the first two components you lay the foundation for a successful sale by learning your account's Buying Process. We'll address the Sales Cycle and the twin relationship sales events and call objectives share—each objective is linked to a sales event. Next, we'll see how to position the first call with new accounts. Positioning yourself with every Key Player is not tricky, but often overlooked.

Yes, we deal with objections in Power Calling. You will handle them with dialogue that will dissolve most objections. Screeners? No returned calls? We work those to our advantage, too. Also, I contend that a powerful voicemail message will take the stale air out of any account, and again, keep the sale moving forward.

Power Calling builds a secure place for your company, which means good business, solid relationships, and repeat customers. Yes! A sale that satisfies you and your account. What is the basis for this success? The prospecting call. The germ of the sale.

In this book, we often refer to a service or opportunity as a product. You will also find we often refer to prospects as accounts or contacts. We generally refer to accounts, contacts, etc. in the masculine. Please rest assured we are neither forgetting nor ignoring the female population. We made the choice of one gender for the purpose of clarity, expedience in expression and in deference to conventional English usage.

Continually refer to your 12 components for ideas, encouragement, advice and inspiration. Have a good time, this is your program, you planned it.

I wish you good fortune and success!
— Joan Guiducci

How do I reach Key Players in the Buying Group?

How are funds released to make the purchase?

How soon will a decision be made?

1

The Buying Process

Putting yourself in the right place, with the right people, at the right time, allows you to make the sale a reality.

That statement may sound obvious, but there are times in sales, we don't know who and how to talk to the people in our accounts. Well, there is a strategic method you can follow that takes away the "surprise" that often occurs when you lose a sale, or are suddenly in the middle of negotiations, and you are dropped out of the loop.

In every company you'll find "the right people," the Key Players. This is the group or committee involved in the decision making. I call this group, the Buying Group. And they carry out, the topic of this first chapter, the Buying Process. As a salesperson, you must be aware of what happens inside a company's ranks before a purchase is approved. It is up to you, the salesperson, to speak with the Buying Group to define the Buying Process within every account, no matter how large or how small. It is essential to build rapport with more than one individual in the account. Very few decisions are made by one person. For example, even if you land a meeting with the President of the United States (an Ultimate Decision Maker), he still must consult his advisers before approving any purchase.

Protect yourself. Don't be the salesperson who cultivates merely one contact within a company and expects to close the sale. If you rely on one person's opinion, you leave yourself wide open for trouble.

Suppose you are selling an accounting system to a company without talking to end-users. You have sold the concept to management, and he passes the product on to his staff for their input. Those employees have the ability to sabotage your sales message during the evaluation process. While some people don't have the authority to say, "yes, we'll buy your product," they can, however, say "no" to your product. It is important to find out who influences the buying decision. Make no assumptions. I have learned this lesson at some expense. In short, talk to all the people who will be involved in using or benefiting from your product (or service) within every account.

Defining Key Players

In most sales, you'll find more than one person in the account affects the Buying Process. These people are the Buying Group made up of Key Players. Throughout the sale you'll want to learn the who, what and how of each Key Player. *Who* means getting the name correct (in spelling and pronunciation), *what* refers to title, and more important than title is *how*. How does each Key Player fit into the company? How does this person affect decisions? How does this person make decisions? The first item on your agenda is to set up a diagram of your Buying Group composed of your Key Players.

Sometimes I draw a wheel. I chose the wheel because it is round, it signifies completion and movement. Choose whatever diagram works for you. In my wheel, the hub represents the Ultimate Decision Maker. Each spoke is a person who will somehow influence the decision to buy or not to buy, each "spoke" may give a green, yellow, or red light toward the purchase. The rim represents the fact that all spokes are related. In order for there to be movement of the sale, I must understand the relationship between each spoke. During a sale, I am travelling around the rim, to the hub, and back around the rim. The more complex the sale, the more "spokes" I'll plan to speak with.

Consider the many Key Players in a company: senior executives, managers, department heads, committee members, accountants, stockholders, end-users, technical specialists, lawyers, engineers, purchasing agents, administrative assistants. Learn how each Key Player fits into the Buying Process. Find the first-line manager. He is usually the person who has access to the senior executives of the company. Cultivate rapport with him, he may be your champion. Find the Ultimate Decision Maker. Find the person who really knows the Buying Process and will share it with you. Find the person who understands the immediate needs of the company. Find the person who sees the long-term growth potential for his company. Work with each person to develop a long-term relationship between your company and his.

TIPSTER

A lot of selling goes on behind the scenes.

The more Key Players you speak to within an organization, the more successful you'll be at signing the business. This is because more people within the account are aware of the benefits of your product or service. Remember, a lot of "selling" goes on while you are not on the line into the account. Key Players can carry your sales message to meetings, to conference calls. The more rapport you have built with each one, the more benefits each player knows, the more likely the sale.

Reaching Key Players

Decide on a logical entry point into the account, then get a contact name and phone number. Look for a contact who has an understanding of the sales potential for the account.

Telephone Talk

At the very least, I would recommend looking for the first-line decision maker. This Key Player has a company-wide perspective of the short-term and long-term needs of his firm. He has credibility with senior management and is a potential high-level champion who can offer suggestions on how to operate with the account. For example, "I would appreciate your advice on talking to the General Manager. How do you see him making the decision? ... What's important to him?" He in turn may become the "inside salesperson" to sell your product to the Ultimate Decision Maker.

But, what is the plan of action when you don't have a contact name or your only choice is an inappropriate entry point into the account? To find the person with whom you need to speak, ask the receptionist for help or find a department within the company that might answer your questions.

Dialogue to get you started:

☎ "Who purchases supplies for the company?"

☎ "Perhaps you can help me. I can't find a name in my files. Who is the Vice President of Sales?"

☎ "I came across a business card for Al Sanders. Is he still the Customer Service Manager?"

☎ "Perhaps, you can help me locate someone in the department."

☎ "I'm not exactly sure if you're the first person I should talk to."

☎ "Who should I talk to about long-term goals for the department?"

☎ "Who would be the best person to start talking with about the safety of your employees?"

Possible entry points, places to find Key Players:

Senior Executive

Sales	Marketing
Telemarketing	Inside Sales
Administration	Customer Service
Operations	Technical Support
Legal	Human Resources

Finance	Accounting
Information Systems	Data Processing
Engineering	Design/Manufacturing
Purchasing	Shipping/Receiving
Warehouse	Distribution

Early in the Sales Cycle, guide calls to a discussion of other Key Players until you've located everyone who can influence the buying decision. Set to work building a list of people influencing the sale, then address their concerns, clarify their opinions. For example, you may say, "I understand you review the monthly report. I'd like to know more about how you use that information, and what other data your department may be looking for."

Start building rapport right away and you'll avoid finding yourself in the awkward position of only courting one person in your account. A word of advice, start this process early in the Sales Cycle. This way, you can comfortably dig for new contacts, and move through the company without slighting anyone. If you wait too long, your "one" contact may feel you are going over his head, or around his back to get what you want.

Dialogue to get you started:
- ☎ "I'd like to get to know everyone involved in the decision."
- ☎ "Who is involved in the decision? What groups are affected?"
- ☎ "Who is on the committee? What departments are represented?"
- ☎ "Could you help me get started with names and phone numbers?"
- ☎ "What's the best time to reach your staff?"
- ☎ "How many locations are involved?"
- ☎ "Which department (end-user) will use this?"
- ☎ "Is there a 'standards' committee?"
- ☎ "Are you responsible for evaluating all products?"
- ☎ "Who is the final decision maker?"
- ☎ "What steps do you go through in making a decision?"
- ☎ "How do you see the decision being made?"
- ☎ "At what level in your organization would this decision be made?"
- ☎ "Who is the project leader? Is it interdepartmental?"

To maintain momentum, contact people as soon as you get their names.

☎ "I'm talking to Don Ride in Customer Service about a new program. He suggested that I talk to you."

☎ "I understand I should talk to you about our plans for customer support. We'd like to find out more about what you need."

What do you do for a living?

I'd like to share an experience that was not so funny at the time, but makes me chuckle when I think of it now. Early in my sales career, when I was selling software by telephone, I started a new position where all the cold accounts were handed to me. I was to take a deep breath and sell, sell, sell. I was instructed to "get a copy of the software into the system manager's office."

Within two weeks, I was successful at getting a sample product into the hands of dozens of "system managers" across my territory. But disaster ensued.

In nearly every case, my definition of a system manager's role did not match the company's definition of the system manager's. He was the custodian of the computer system. I had been dealing with people who were not quite at the level I needed. And to tell you the truth, I think I knew it all along. For some reason, I ignored that voice tugging inside me (which I now listen to!). Basically, my mistake was failing to ask my contact three critical questions:

- What is your role as system manager?
- Who else is involved in this decision?
- How do you see the decision being made?

I lost precious time catching up with all my test sites. But I did and it was a lesson well-learned. The moral of the foible? Talk to everyone involved in the decision. And always ask a contact just how he fits into the organization.

Discuss roles to gain understanding of how the organization makes decisions. Learn 1) how Key Players interact, 2) how each influences the Buying Process, and 3) the issues important to each Key Player.

Dialogue to get you started:

☎ "Tell me how Customer Service and Engineering interact?"

☎ "Who reads the sales report?"

☎ "What branch offices are affected by the installation?"

☎ "Who would you call if you had a problem or question?"

☎ "Who handles implementation?"

☎ "Who should I talk to about the accounting system?"

☎ "What is the selection process?"

☎ "What is the structure of your organization?"

☎ "What is 'legal's' role?"

☎ "Who cuts the purchase order?"

☎ "How do you fit into the organization?"

☎ "What are your priorities in Customer Service?"

☎ "It would really help to understand your role as the Administrator."

☎ "What is the structure for the project?"

☎ "What is the goal of the evaluator?"

☎ "Do you know the goals of the other committee members?"

☎ "Where are the largest number of workstations?"

☎ "Who should I keep advised of the progress we're making?"

☎ "Who do you rely on to keep you informed about training needs?"

☎ "Who can say "no" to the decision?"

☎ "Who could potentially stop this sale?"

☎ "Is the decision influenced by another location?"

☎ "What factors influence the final buying decision?"

☎ "Are you talking to other suppliers?"

☎ "What are you trying to accomplish?"

☎ "How are you planning to implement this?"

☎ "What criteria are you using to make this decision?"

☎ "What is important to you? Other Key Players?"

☎ "Where is the decision made?"

☎ "Is this a department or a company decision?"

Telephone Talk

TIPSTER

The more people within the account who are aware of the benefits of your product, the more successful you'll be.

Rehearse with Key Players to sell the benefits of your proposal to the Ultimate Decision Maker in case you are not in the position to make the presentation yourself.

Court the champions

A champion is an insider who stands to gain something—prestige, or perhaps recognition from supporting your sales message and carrying it to other Key Players. Your product or service helps him in some way. Thus, your champion works on your behalf selling in the background, when you are not on site or on the telephone. Keep your champion advised of the sales' progress; use him as a reference. Go to him for advice. Cultivate one strong ally in every account.

☎ "We're making good progress. I'd like to fill you in."

☎ "I would really appreciate your thoughts on this."

☎ "Something has come up that you may want to know about."

Who signs the dotted line?

Learn about the budget. Locate the individual who gives the final "yes" because he is the Ultimate Decision Maker. Suppose you encounter a committee delegated to making the buying decision. Chances are you'll discover there is still only one individual who gives the final "yes" because he is the Ultimate Decision Maker.

Dialogue to get you started:

☎ "Who controls the budget?"

☎ "Who releases funds to make the purchase?"

☎ "Who gives the final approval for the sale?"

☎ "Is there money in the budget?"

☎ "What is your budget for the project?"

☎ "Are you responsible for setting (forecasting) the budget? Time frame?"

☎ "Do you control the budget for the project?"

☎ "What happens if we're over budget?"
☎ "Do you have money to spend now?"
☎ "Have your budgeted for this product?"

How soon will a decision be made?"

Learn about the buyer's time frame early in the Sales Cycle to help you prioritize your selling activity within the account.

Dialogue to get you started:
☎ "How soon will a decision be made?"
☎ "How much time do you need to make the evaluation?"
☎ "When do you expect to hear back from the user group?"
☎ "When should he get involved in the decision?"
☎ "When do you expect to hear about the decision for the proposal?"
☎ "How soon will you turn over your recommendations?"
☎ "Have you made a decision?"
☎ "When will the pilot roll out?"
☎ "What is the scope of the pilot?"
☎ "What is the process after a product has been chosen?"
☎ "When do you think the decision process will begin?"

TIPSTER
Elicit help from
Key Players for
your meeting with
the Ultimate
Decision Maker.

Action Plan

Key Players

1) From the list in this chapter, choose which departments and Key Players are relevant to your account.

2) Learn each Key Player's role.

3) Write the questions you might ask to locate other Key Players.

4) Write the questions you might ask to learn the time frame and budget.

On a final note...

Exercise caution when prospecting by telephone. You can't always see the lay of the land, so consistently confirm who the Key Players are and what role they serve in the account.

Gain the confidence of everyone who can say "no" to the buying decision. Find out how Key Players influence the purchase.

Search at the appropriate corporate level for the person who actually makes the decision.

TIPSTER
Cultivate
relationships with
champions, you
can never have
too many.

How do I manage accounts step-by-step
toward a buying decision?

What is the right time and sequence to
contact Key Players?

2

The Sales Cycle • Selling Events

Knowing the Sales Cycle helps you forecast your accounts and manage your selling time.

Chances are you have some understanding of the time frame needed and the steps necessary to close a sale. This makes up the Sales Cycle. Once you have a lead in hand, it usually begins with planning a strategy for the first call into the account, and ends with post-sale follow-up. Naturally, the length of time and number of steps depends upon what product or service you are selling. You may even have more than one distinct Sales Cycle. For example, your Sales Cycle may differ according to the types of products you offer, or you may find the complexity and time frame increases as the dollar amount of the sale also rises. Regardless, the process of building the Sales Cycle is the same.

First, you will find the account's Key Players. Then you will organize the steps necessary to move through the sale. I call these steps, "Selling Events." The more intimate your knowledge of your Selling Events, the more adept you are at structuring your selling time and managing your accounts. This means more accurate forecasts to your sales manager!

The Sales Cycle is a timeline of Selling Events. Every sales event is attached to a sales call (either by telephone, or in person) with a Key Player. Each call has an objective: to accomplish a Selling Event.

Managing accounts step-by-step toward a buying decision

Consider every account a "project." Designate yourself the project manager responsible for coordinating the entire sales process. Talk to Key Players on a regular schedule so you know where you stand within the account. The more effective you are managing the account's progress, the more efficient you are closing the business. Hence, a shorter Sales Cycle and a quicker sale.

When planning your approach to an account, consider all stages of the sale no matter how obscure or trivial. Be sure to touch all bases from beginning to end. Detail every step in writing and keep an eye on each Selling Event.

Here is a sample timeline, listing stages of a Sales Cycle to help you get started: 1) pre-qualify account 2) identify Buying Group, 3) develop need, 4) demonstrate product capability, 5) summarize benefits, 6) offer solution, 7) prove need, 8) obtain commitment to purchase, 9) agree to terms and conditions, 10) take order.

Next, break down these stages even further into specific Selling Events. If you are working a simple sale, you may be able to accomplish several stages in a single Selling Event. Or, a complex sale may require multiple Selling Events to complete a single stage because of all the Key Players involved.

Selling Events to get you started:
 Make initial contact
 Determine Key Players in the Buying Group
 Contact Key Players
 Learn needs (qualifying process)
 Send product literature
 Send/install evaluation
 Send/deliver samples
 Offer references
 Provide demonstration
 Submit proposal
 Review proposal
 Negotiate contract
 Get commitment
 Get contract signed
 Take order
 Post-sale support

Contact Key Players: When and in what order?

Now that you have strategically mapped your Selling Events, you are
nearly ready to begin working your sales strategy with Key Players. Call
Key Players as soon as you acquire their names. If you ask the right questions, you'll find Key Players can help you build the Sales Cycle and define Selling Events.

On your initial call to each Key Player, investigate the decision-
making process to determine where he belongs in the Sales Cycle. To
drive sales toward the close, probe Key Players to discover what they will
need to make a decision and how much time it takes to accomplish each
step.

Dialogue to get you started:
☎ "How do you see the decision being made?"
☎ "What happens after the evaluation?"

☎ "What is the "final" decision maker looking for?"
☎ "What issues are important to management?"
☎ "What role does purchasing play in the decision?"
☎ "How much time do you need to examine the product?"
☎ "What is your schedule for implementing the new system?"
☎ "How much time does purchasing need to process the order?"
☎ "Do you have funds in your budget?"

Call Objectives

To determine the objective of your sales call, ask yourself, "What am I trying to make happen in this account and how do I accomplish it on this call?"

TIPSTER

Key Players may tell you their role in the Sales Cycle. Just ask.

For example:

Pre-qualify account

Establish need

Locate a contact name

Learn about the account's Buying Process

Determine the budget and timeline for a project

Set appointment

Confirm appointment

Commitment to review literature

Set telephone date to review literature

Get agreement for an evaluation

Start evaluation

Arrange demonstration

Complete demonstration

Register someone for an event

Present references

Get funds released

Take an order

Get commitment

Get signed contract

Building the Sales Cycle

The following is a sample Sales Cycle. To clarify this particular Sales Cycle, I've divided it into three parts: pre-qualify, evaluation, close. During this particular case, we are talking to the first-line decision maker and the evaluator. An evaluator is the person who is examining or analyzing your product or service. He is the person setting requirements, and making sure the product meets those specifications. The evaluator is usually the one who has hands-on experience with your product, and may request a demonstration or sample. This person may even consider placing a small order early in the Sales Cycle.

1. Pre-qualify
Preliminary qualifying process and needs analysis

Ideal Entry Point: First-Line Decision Maker

This Key Player has a global understanding and company-wide perspective of short-term and long-term needs of his firm. He has credibility with high-level management (e.g., final decision maker and other committee members). For you, the sales person, he is a potential high-level champion who can offer advice and direction on how to operate within his company. He can often direct you to the evaluator of products.

Selling Event: Pre-qualify sales potential of the account by assessing immediate need and long-term growth of the company.

Call Objective: Obtain commitment for product evaluation.

Questions I must answer:

TIPSTER

Intimate knowledge of Selling Events allows for more accurate sales forecasting.

- What does the account know and think about our company?
- Does the account have an immediate need?
- What is the account's long-term plan?
- What is the current environment and competition?
- Can I coexist with other suppliers?
- What is the Buying Process?
- Who are the Key Players?
- Where do I go from here?

Dialogue to get you started:

☎ "How familiar are you with our company?"

☎ "Have you ever used our products? ... If so, which ones?"

☎ "What are the top five priorities for your organization for this fiscal year?"

☎ "What are your strategies/plans for this year?"

☎ "Tell me about your current supplier. What do you like best?"

☎ "Tell me about your current environment."

☎ "Who determines and supports standards for the company? ... Does your group mandate standards or do you only make the recommendation?"

☎ "Who else needs to be involved in the decision?"

☎ "What role does purchasing play in the decision and purchasing cycle? ... Can they stop an order if you have budget available or do they normally fulfill orders for you?"

☎ "Who conducts the evaluation? ... Does he report directly to you?"

☎ "What is the general time frame for an evaluation? ... Once the evaluation is complete, what does it take to make a decision and move the order through the company? ... How much time do you need?"

☎ "Are products purchased centrally by your group for the company, or do individual business units have their own budgets? ... If individual groups purchase, do you have any influence over what they choose or evaluate? Is budget available for the purchase?"

Next, you will move to the "Evaluator." This person is critical. He is not a decision maker, yet he can say "no" to a buying decision. Generally, the evaluator possesses detailed knowledge of standards, your competition, requirements he would like fulfilled, and problem areas which need addressing. He has credibility with direct management as an expert. (Keep in mind, the evaluator may have his or her own agenda to fulfill. Be on the lookout for these clues. Your evaluator may be a champion or a saboteur.)

Key Player: Evaluator
Selling Event: Build a relationship with the evaluator. Learn the evaluation process and gather more details on the current needs.
Call Objective: Obtain commitment to start the evaluation.

Dialogue to get you started:

☎ "How familiar are you with our company? ... What do you like best about what you know?"

☎ "Have you used our products before? ... If so, what do you like best about them?"

☎ "What do you use as criteria for an evaluation?"

☎ "Do you have a checklist? ... If so may I take a look at it?"

☎ "Is there anyone else I should speak to about this evaluation?"

☎ "Who else is involved in the decision?"

☎ "Do you report directly to the first-line decision maker?"

☎ "Who sets your priorities?"

☎ "What other products are you considering for this evaluation? ... Have you used any of these products before? ... If so, which ones? ... What do you think of them?"

☎ "What are the key issues you are trying to address with the product? ... What features are important to you? ... Do you have a current standard in this product category? ... If yes, is your current product performing to your standards?"

☎ "How would you rank the importance of the following factors: company longevity, product features, support, pricing, etc.? ... Which of these factors impact the decision to purchase?"

☎ "When can you start the evaluation?"

☎ "How long does it take to conduct an evaluation? ...What support do you need from us during the evaluation?"

☎ "When the evaluation is complete, to whom do you report the results?"

TIPSTER

Keep in touch with Key Players on a regular schedule.

2. Evaluation • Examination • Needs Analysis
Develop needs and prove solution

Key Player: Evaluator

Selling Events: Get issues and questions resolved and prove that the product meets specifications.

Call Objectives: Get evaluation started, hold the account's hand and begin showing how product meets specification.

Dialogue to get you started:

☎ "Did you get the evaluation?"

☎ "Are you on schedule to start tomorrow?"

☎ "Do you have any questions?"

☎ "Are you having any problems?"

☎ "Have you thought about implementation?"

☎ "You can call me with any questions."

☎ "This is the level of support you can count on from us."

☎ "How do you see this product helping you?"

☎ "When do you meet with your manager? ... Are you going to talk about the evaluation? ..What are your thoughts?"

Key Player: First-Line Decision Maker

Selling Event: Report on initial status of the evaluation.

Call Objective: Advise that the evaluation has successfully started.

☎ "I understand the evaluation is successfully underway. What have you heard?"

Key Player: Evaluator

Selling Events: Hold the evaluator's hand, and continue to develop need.

Call Objective: Learn how evaluation does or does not meet requirements.

Dialogue to get you started:

☎ "How is the evaluation going?"

☎ "What do you like best about the product?"

☎ "Does the product meet specification?"

☎ "Is the evaluation on schedule?"

☎ "How do you see this helping you?"

☎ "Are you going to complete the evaluation on schedule?"

☎ "What is your recommendation?"

☎ "How does our product compare to your current supplier?"

☎ "What do you like best about us?"

Key Player: First-Line Decision Maker
Selling Event: Offer to report the status of the evaluation. Continue clari-
fying time frame and budget required to make a decision.
Call Objectives: Agree on the progress of the evaluation and continue
need analysis. Offer references.

Dialogue to get you started:

☎ "Here's our perspective of the evaluation. Do you agree?"

☎ "The evaluation is going well. This is how I see our product helping your organization. Perhaps, you would like to talk to our customers."

☎ "Is there a budget available to make the purchase?"

☎ "What is the purchasing process? .. How soon should we get
started?"

　　　　See the process of detailing Selling Events? Break down the
stages of the Sales Cycle, then plug in Key Players one accomplishment
at a time.

3. The Close
Obtaining commitment and processing the order

Key Player: First-Line Decision Maker
Selling Event: Obtain commitment on the need and "rehearse" him to sell the solution to the final decision maker.
Call Objectives: Obtain commitment to purchase.
Dialogue to get you started:

☎ **"I understand the evaluator agrees this product addresses your needs, improves your situation."**

☎ **"I'd like to help you with the presentation for the Ultimate Decision Maker. What do you need?"**

Key Player: "Final" Decision Maker
Selling Event: Present solution.
Call Objectives: Obtain commitment to purchase.

Key Player: Purchasing and Legal
Selling Event: Negotiate final pricing, terms and conditions, and contract.
Call Objective: Obtain commitment from purchasing and legal departments.

Action Plan

The Sales Cycle
1) List Sales Events in the order they are most likely to happen.

2) List corresponding call objectives.

3) List Key Players including their roles, and what you plan to accomplish on each call.

On a final note...

Probe Key Players so you understand the Sales Cycle and define Selling Events.

Your success is determined by how well you set call objectives.

Concentrate on specific accomplishments that move you closer to a buying decision.

TIPSTER
Knowing the
Sales Cycle gives
you a reliable tool
for defining the
objective of every
sales call.

Who are the ideal accounts?

What is the most effective approach for finding ideal accounts?

How can I leverage my current accounts for more business?

3

Target Markets •Lead Sources

Pinpoint ideal accounts by prioritizing leads that award the best payoff, with the least amount of effort, in the shortest amount of time.

Your goal is to make new business contacts through telephone prospecting. If you don't devise a strategy for finding your ideal accounts, you're bound to waste a lot of time. After all, if you're hunting for deer, you don't wade through the duck pond.

And yet this is what many salespeople do on a daily basis. Often, when we start a position with a company, we are given a territory and a database of leads. Our leads come from many sources. The list may be built according to criteria or targeted demographics defined by your company. Seems like a great setup until we look at the overwhelming hundreds or thousands of names in front of us. Where do we begin? At "A" and work our way to "Z" by the end of the year? Snooze. No, of course not.

This chapter is designed to get you thinking about efficient use your prospecting time and resources. The following strategies will add value to your selling hours and numbers to your sales volume.

Defining your Target Markets

Find accounts that look like your past and current customers to get maximum value from your selling experience using the Target Market approach.

"What's all this talk about Target Markets? "you ask. "My company has a niche. My ideal account is everybody on my list." Sure, many company products and services fulfill a niche, but a Target Market in my definition is different. A Target Market is a smaller pocket of success within your niche.

I am urging you to define Target Markets in addition to the niche marketing your company may be pursuing. And, of course, if you don't already have a specific niche or a product for a specific industry, your only logical choice is to define your Target Markets.

The concept behind Target Markets is more effective than you might think. What you need to do is focus on where you've had successful sales. That is where your experience lies. For example, if you are a stockbroker, you may believe everyone out there who has a portfolio is an ideal account. However, if you look at the portfolios you work with today and see many of your clients are in certain professions, perhaps you might look at them as your Target Markets. If you sell a software change control system for an IBM Midrange Computer, you may think that anyone who owns that model is an account—until you research your current customers and notice many of them are banks. Perhaps you could then say that Financial Institutions subject to government regulations is a Target Market.

Give this approach a try, and you'll notice your experience from one account carries over to the next. You are speaking the account's language. Due to your experience in his field, you can help the account achieve his goals because you understand his needs. You have an idea of how their organization is designed, i.e., you have research from past ex-

TIPSTER

Devise a plan for finding your ideal accounts. Otherwise you're bound to waste a lot of time.

perience about who Key Players are and how they fit into the Buying Process. You can provide a list of satisfied customers. Your account will feel comfortable with you right away and you will feel more comfortable calling him. Bingo. A smoother, quicker sale.

Back to the source

Use sources that give you the best results with the least number of phone calls, to reach the best opportunities in the shortest amount of time. If you are new to a company, talk to other salespeople, your colleagues, your sales manager for research.

TIPSTER

Use the
Target Market
approach
for smoother,
quicker sales.

You may be using a company-supplied list. This is fine, but experience shows that building your own list over time holds the most value. To do this, keep an eye out for new developments in your territory or industry. For example, let's say you sell commercial security systems. You may look in the news for places or industries that fall prey to burglaries.

Or, if you are an outplacement employment company, you may look for companies where profits are down and rightsizing is leading to closed branches. Also in this case, you may be on the lookout for companies merging and thereby putting more people in the job market, which you can help to place.

Simply put, pay attention to business trends that can signal a market for you to tap into.

Review the list below and make notes about which sources result in the most amount of sales.

Company-supplied leads from:
    Advertising campaign
    Direct mailers
    Incoming calls
    Trade shows or conferences
Company-supplied lists
Networking group
Exchanging leads with other people
Current clients

Referrals
Canvassing businesses
Professional associations
Magazines, journals
Membership lists
List publisher or broker
On-line service or database
Local or national directories
     Standard and Poor's
     Dun and Bradstreet
     Thomas Directory
Telephone directory
Reverse or criss-cross directories
Newspapers
     Business sections
     Personal announcements
     Classified advertisements

TIPSTER

Look to companies that are growing so you can grow with them.

Rapport and Referral

Ask for referrals and look for people willing to exchange leads. Look to current customers for repeat sales to capitalize on your past efforts in developing the business relationship. Ask them for new contacts within the account.

If you have been building rapport with Key Players within your accounts, you may feel comfortable asking for referrals from them. Most business people are willing to exchange leads. Most savvy people know what goes around comes around. One good deed paves the way for another. If you believe in your product or service and have worked in some post-sales support, it is very proper to look to a current customer for repeat sales. Build more business from the footwork you have already accomplished.

Present new ideas to "old" contacts. Talk about new developments with dissatisfied customers or lost business to rekindle interest in your product or service.

Ask current customers about their suppliers. Look for contacts that share similar Target Markets. Give them a call. Perhaps, you can help each other.

Dialogue to get you started:

☎ "A mutual acquaintance of ours, Mark West, says you're one of the best in your business. I'd like to talk over an idea. Perhaps we can help each other."

☎ "Are you still using the Model 3300? ... I'd like to talk over a couple of ideas."

☎ "I came across a business card for Al Sanders. Is he still the Customer Service Manager?"

☎ "It's been nearly six months since we've talked. Are there any changes?"

☎ "It's been awhile since we've talked. We've made some changes I think could help you organize all your microfilm more efficiently."

☎ "Does each division have its own sales department? ... Do they operate independently of each other? ... Do you know what they are doing about these issues? ... Where do you suggest I start?"

☎ "It occurred to me you might know other people I could talk to."

☎ "We're working with other hospitals."

☎ "We're interested in hearing how you're doing."

☎ "I've studied your account and I have some ideas that can improve turnaround time on your color printing."

☎ "I noticed something in the news and thought of you."

☎ "We really value your opinion. We're interested in your reaction to a new service."

☎ "I realized we've never really talked about your packaging needs."

☎ "I remembered you mentioned the new organization would be decided this month. How's that going?"

☎ "We've made some changes to our product line you may want to know about."

☎ "I know you were disappointed in our service, but we've made some changes."

TIPSTER

Relate your experience in his field and your account will feel more comfortable with you.

Action Plan

Target Markets

1) List specific accounts with whom you've had experience. Which were successful sales that brought satisfied customers? Is there a common denominator? Does it have Target Market potential?

2) Here are some ideas for describing your ideal accounts:
Ask yourself, "What criteria will most ideal accounts meet?"

For example:
Industries/type of business
Common need or problem to solve
Size of company
Number of employees
Annual sales
Number of locations
Specific type of contact
Specific buying habits
What events would signal a purchase
Related products or services used by my ideal account

On a final note...

You can often shorten your Sales Cycle by selling into accounts that look like your satisfied customers.

Start with leads that come from your best source.

Accounts will feel more interested in talking to you if you have some understanding of their business.

TIPSTER
Lists
you build for
your business
have the
most value.

How do I get maximum value from my calls?

What must I do to prepare this presentation?

What am I trying to make happen in this account right now?

4

Call Strategies •Account Planning

Organizing Target Markets and planning your moves in advance makes for the most effective presentation on every call.

If you have followed suggestions in the Power Calling approach so far, your lead list is now prioritized and categorized according to Target Markets. What is the next move?

The questions I hear most are, "What is the best opening line to use? How long is the typical first call to a contact? And how should I close the call?" What people are really asking me is, "How do I get the most from every call?" I have a straightforward answer. Successful Call Strategies and Account Planning means relating your product to your Target Markets, using time wisely, setting call objectives, and reaching call objectives.

Look where you've been

The way to form your strategy and then plan the actions you'll take to your accounts is found within your selling history. (If you are new to your company, or to sales, look to a colleague's past experience.)

Rather than rushing forward, step back and look at what you are doing. The stones paving the road to your success are called evaluation and re-evaluation. Study your current ways of doing things. Study your ideal accounts.

The way to achieve most Power Calling methods is to ask yourself a question. In this case, the question is, "Where have I been successful before and why?"

Use a production-line approach

Surely the amount of time you spend on weekly prospecting is important, but how you spend that time is critical.

In the last chapter we discussed Target Markets and how they help you leverage your lead sources. Now, let's expand the discussion of Target Markets to include how they help you get not only the most from every prospecting session, but from every call.

Make all your calls for each Target Market in the same time block. This makes for quality prospecting time and a "tighter" presentation. Why? You are talking to the same type of accounts facing similar issues. You are familiar with the Key Player's dialogue. Each conversation you have builds a foundation for the next call you make into a different account. This builds your confidence and in turn builds your account's confidence in you. Also, you will spend less time preparing for each individual call, because you understand the difficulties these types of accounts are facing.

Now back to the questions. "Where have I been successful and why?" Identify past and present satisfied customers that experienced similar difficulties in their workday. And then ask yourself these questions to prepare a Call Strategy for each Target Market:

• What industry knowledge do I have that can help these accounts accomplish their goals?

- What selling experience can I relate to this Target Market?
- What problems does my product solve?
- What's my solution?
- What results are customers experiencing?
- What role do Key Players serve?
- What competition shares this Target Market with me?
- How do they stand out? How is my solution better?

Action gets the account moving

This brings us to a discussion of Account Planning. Set your Target Market strategy in front of you. Set your lead in front of you. What do you know about the account that can help you? What information do you have in your files? Have you spoken to the account previously?

There may be times you want to research your account. Call for annual reports, or make calls outside the Buying Group to get answers that can pre-qualify the account. For example, "Perhaps you can help me. How many employees are there at this branch office?" Every bit of background information you have gives you an edge.

Take notes before you dial. Prospecting means you are calling "them" and that puts you in control. Log that desk time so that once you're on the phone, you'll have everything you need to make an effective presentation. Prepare before each call. Refer to your Sales Cycle. Review your research. Your notes should include this information:

Target Market
Date
Lead source
Contact
Title/role
Telephone
Fax
Company
Address
Type of business
Call objective

TIPSTER

Make calls outside
the Buying Group
to pre-qualify
the account.

Secondary objective
What you know about the account
Items to address/questions you will ask
Potential problems/solutions/results
Other Key Players
Name
Title/role
Telephone number

Setting call objectives

In the chapter on the Sales Cycle, we talked about your goal of keeping the sale moving toward the close, how each call is an integral part of that movement. So aim for a specific action that involves a commitment from the account. Ask yourself, "What exactly am I trying to make happen in this account right now? What is the objective of my call?"

The content of your call is determined by your call objective, which you must define before dialing the phone number. For example, are you introducing yourself, setting an appointment, gathering information, conducting an interview or survey, sending literature for follow-up, or determining an account's budget for a project? Naturally, the accomplishment of each goal dictates the time frame needed for your conversation.

Map your questions so that the conversation opens and closes where you want it to. Be alert for signs of resistance, or conversely, commitment. Depending on circumstances, avoid discussing too much on the first call. Accomplish your objective and then hang up. Be sure to leave your account feeling good about hearing from you again.

If you review the list below, you'll see that it echoes the list of Selling Events in Chapter 2. Get the idea? Each call accomplishes a Selling Event, moving you through the Sales Cycle, one step, one call at a time. Notice how many times you may be talking to the account—it is this repeated and consistent contact that builds a solid business relationship!

TIPSTER

Make all your calls to each Target Market in the same time block.

Ideas to get you started

Pre-qualify account

Establish need

Locate a contact name

Learn about the account's buying process

Determine the budget and timeline for a project

Set appointment

Confirm appointment

Commitment to review literature

Set telephone date to review literature

Get agreement for an evaluation

Start evaluation

Arrange demonstration

Complete demonstration

Register someone for an event

Present references

Get funds released

Take an order

Get commitment

Get signed contract

TIPSTER

Strategy
is a prerequiste to
your success.

Organize your facts in such a way that you heighten your account's interest in your sales message. Be sure to have an alternate objective in case your first goes awry.

Let's replay what your calls may sound like.

Before you made the call, did you ask yourself two important questions?

• What am I trying to make happen in this account?

• How do I accomplish it with this telephone call?

If you have answered these questions (and I gently insist you put them on paper), then you will be planning action in your account through smart call strategies.

Action Plan

Defining A Target Market

1) List three potential problems (challenges) your products can solve (or improve).

2) Identify past and present customers that experienced these difficulties.

TIPSTER

Show the account how your selling experience can help achieve his goals.

3) Note the line of questioning you used to help customers understand their situations.

4) Describe the solution or improvement your product offers.

5) List "typical" Key Players in this Target Market.

Determining Call Objectives

1) Refer to the list in this chapter to define objectives relative to your Sales Cycle.

2) Prepare an action plan for each Key Player you listed above.

On a final note...

A goal without a plan is only a wish.

Strategy is a prerequisite to your success during the call.

Plan an approach for each Target Market so you don't have to repeat the same process every time you call those types of accounts.

You may feel uneasy about a call if you're unclear about what you want to accomplish.

The amount of time you spend prospecting is important, but how you spend that time is critical.

TIPSTER

Avoid discussing

too much

on the

first call.

What are the advantages of doing business with our company?

How can the account use our product to improve his situation?

What is the appropriate presentation for each Key Player?

5

Selling Solutions • Solving Problems

Matching the end results of your product to the needs expressed by the account delivers a powerful sales message.

Sometimes we just don't know where to start "selling" to an account. Do we work with big picture ideas? Or do we get down to details and discuss the most advanced bells and whistles our product offers? Before we ask ourselves where to start, let's explore what points add the most value to our sales message on the first call to a contact.

Consider talking to satisfied or repeat customers about why they do business with you or your company. They'll tell you why they buy from you. They'll tell the results they're experiencing. How did they select you over your competition or their current supplier? If you coexist with other suppliers, how do you compare? What are the advantages of doing business with your company? Listen to their perspective. Note their comments and use their language to build your repertoire of key phrases.

Integrate this vocabulary into your conversations. Put the advantages at the forefront of your dialogue. For example, "... another way we can help is cutting down on travel time and reducing expenses because we have a support center close to each of your branch offices."

Use every resource. Look into your company's collateral. Highlight statements that can help you make important points about your company or product. This will help you build benefit statements. Keep in mind the idea of partnership between you and your account. Together you are working toward solutions. For example, "I work exclusively in the county, so I'm no stranger to the limitations on new construction, but we have been able to get other projects like yours approved." Or, "I'm current on the recent laws, so I'm able to you tell you their impact on your business."

Legwork is crucial to building your story. Read trade journals, related newspaper articles, everything you can find that relates or even seems to relate to what you are selling. Listen to what others in your industry are saying. Attend conferences and seminars. This way, you are not just another salesperson selling a product, you become a consultant, an expert in the field.

Find consultative words to describe your company or product. Here is a group of words that I choose from to get my story started: specialize, expertise, well-known, shorten, accomplished, connections, creative, unique, innovative, recent, new, proven, industry-standard, enhance, reliable, streamline, effective, efficient, accurate, selection, choice, flexible, control, opportunity, stronger, productive, improve, replace, growth, powerful, easy, time-saver, faster, speed, quickly, increase, growing, more, less, fewer, eliminate, reduce, equal, savings, results, affordable, fair, reasonable, value, total quality, and so on.

TIPSTER

Make sure Key Players can explain benefits of your product to each other.

Improving a situation

Organize the end results your product can provide. You may be familiar with the feature-advantage-benefit routine. To determine what benefits to play up, look for the applied value of each feature of your company and product. How can you improve the situation for the department, the company? Is yours stronger, faster, safer, more affordable? How does it affect the account's working conditions or bottom line? How can you support the account?

For example:

• You are on the leading edge, an innovator in your field. You can pass savings on to the customer.

☎ **"We've developed an innovative program that can lower stress levels for production line workers, and reduce worker's compensation insurance costs."**

☎ **"Our specialty is helping manufacturers improve the output of finished goods. We now have a cost-effective way to install the process at plants with your volume levels."**

• Your product can help the account get back on schedule and stay within his budget.

☎ **"You'll also be glad to know this can take even more pressure off your staff. They won't need to interrupt their work day."**

☎ **"This can control costs by reducing the number of man-hours needed to take care of ..."**

• You have outstanding support.

☎ **"You'll find our help desk useful. We also operate 24 hours a day, so when you need that support after hours you can talk to a technician right away. You won't have to wait until the following day for help like you do now."**

• Your product or service is one of the "best" in the industry.

☎ **"Our utensils have been used in hospital kitchens for nearly 30 years. We're well-known for the quality materials we use and for the life time warranty."**

One technique I use to be sure I am explaining the value, is by asking myself, "How is that feature important to the account?"

For example:

☎ **"This helps them to take more calls, and the big plus for your people is they'll feel more relaxed at the end of the day."**

☎ **"On the issue of our distribution centers, we spend millions each year so you don't have to be concerned about getting behind in your operation. We're always current with the latest technology."**

Now that we asked, "Why is that important to the account?" Let's ask, "How does it specifically relate to the account's situation?" Don't be content to merely add words such as savings, faster, easier, or better in your benefit statements. People are always looking to save time and money, but what specifically is affecting budget and schedule?

In the following example, notice how you can get more interesting and visual by getting specific with benefit statements. For example, "And because of the compiling capabilities, you'll be able shorten development time by at least 30%. That can take some pressure off the overtime problem, and you can still meet your deadline. Your people don't have to learn a lot of new techniques because we're compatible with ...."

Get started describing major points of your company. Build statements that highlight your expertise and specialty. Be sure to add comments from satisfied customers.

Dialogue to get you started:

☎ **"And we have over 1,000 companies in town using the program because of our response time. We guarantee ...."**

☎ **"We're good at developing other people's ideas into a tangible product."**

☎ **"You may know of us from the work we did for ...."**

☎ "Our new accounts are often referred to us by our customers."

☎ "You may have heard about a new .... We're involved."

☎ "We specialize in working with companies ...."

☎ "We're expert at helping our clients ...."

☎ "We work with our clients on improving their ...."

☎ "I'd like to tell you a little bit about who we are and what we do."

☎ "Since we don't know each other, I'd like to tell you about myself and the kind of work I do."

Because you know your product or service intimately, you may feel it's time to get on the phone with your priority leads chosen from your Target Markets and let it rip, right? Not so soon.

The method of discussing all the impressive product features during the call, hoping the account will pick one that applies, is not the most efficient way to grab and hold your account's attention. No matter how enthusiastic you are about features and benefits, they will mean little until you translate them into living examples which appeal to your account's needs.

First, you must spend time finding out specifically what challenges are facing the account. This is true especially if you believe you understand the account's needs before ever talking to him. Recall the old adage. Assume nothing. We discussed earlier, we are trying to anticipate unnecessary surprises that may crop up at each stage of the sale.

Relating to your account

While drawing the blueprints for the Buying Process and Sales Cycle, your assignment is to find out what issues are important to each Key Player. What does he care about? What area is he struggling with in his department? What situation needs improving? What elements create crucial moments during the day?

Keep in mind the account is asking himself these two questions: 1) What can your product do for me? 2) How will your product work for me?

He wants to hear relevant and specific product capabilities and benefits. Be aware of subtle differences in word choice. For example, rather than saying, "This can help if you have trouble keeping trained people." Be more certain of his goals and concerns. The following statement is more concrete and convincing. "This can help with the training issues you are concerned about, so you always have a capable operator." See the difference?

After you have a good feel for his needs then you can direct the conversation to your product. For example, "You made an important point earlier that I'd like to talk more about. We have a way to ...." After growing familiar with an account's daily difficulties, you can assure with solid confidence your recommendation can take care of his concern.

For example:
☎ **"And another way this will help you is ...."**
☎ **"You'll find ... useful ...."**
☎ **"And because of ... you can also ...."**
☎ **"And another way we can improve performance ...."**
☎ **"This will give you what you want."**

Focus on specific solutions and the account will gain enthusiasm for your product. Make sure Key Players are comfortable explaining the benefits of your product to each other. Keep in mind that you are solving a problem, or improving a situation.

TIPSTER

People buy
from you
when they buy
what you are
selling.

More dialogue to get you started:
☎ **"You need delivery in a hurry, we can send product from our warehouse the same day when you order by noon. We can also eliminate steps by putting you onto our network, and then you can place orders directly from your workstation."**
☎ **"From what you're saying about the affects of the reorganization, you would see a big improvement with company morale with our ...."**
☎ **"You'll be pleased to hear about the speed because it's more efficient than your current workstation."**

Relate a similar environment that makes it easy for the account to understand your product, and your sales message will have a longer lasting impact. For example: "I've talked to other non profit organizations about fund-raising. This is what they're doing to improve their results."

Speak the contact's language

It is essential you tailor each presentation according to each Key Player's role! For example, an end user cares most about product capabilities and ease of use, a first-line manager cares more about productivity, and the Ultimate Decision Maker is concerned with budget, i.e., will the solution ultimately cost less than the problem?

In large organizations you'll find Key Players have standard roles. The smaller the company, the more likely Key Players are assuming more than one role, wearing more hats, if you will. Generally, people at the front line are concerned with day-to-day detail. As you move up in the organization's ladder, Key Players have a broader and longer-term vision of the company's needs. The difference is perspective. For example:

Ultimate decision maker:

☎ **"We have new techniques that can cut design time by 30% or more. That takes care of reducing the overtime costs you're concerned about. And because we're compatible with your current system, you can do the installation without interrupting your production schedule."**

First-line manager:

☎ **"You'll also be glad to hear this can take more pressure off your staff. They won't need to interrupt work schedules to learn a lot of new techniques because we're compatible with your current system. This can help with your concern about making your development deadline."**

End user:

☎ **"You won't have to wait like you do now, because the compiler can assemble all of your records in under five minutes. And because we're compatible with your current system, you won't have to learn a lot of new techniques."**

53

Action Plan

Your company, your product

1) Call three customers and ask them to describe the advantages of doing business with your company.

2) Look at your account. For each Key Player describe possible problems and the solution your product brings to him. Focus on major features and capabilities.

3) Describe your company and expertise in 100 words or less.

On a final note...

You will have a more positive impact by describing the value of your product rather than how it works.

Make sure Key Players selling on your behalf understand the benefits.

Accounts are more likely to remember your product if you describe familiar scenes related to their business.

Speak the account's language. Get technical only after they ask technical questions.

TIPSTER

Focus on
specific solutions.
Your account
will gain
enthusiasm
for your product.

What is the account's situation?

Does the account perceive dissatisfaction, difficulties, or problems in his work day?

What are the buying signals?

6

Developing Need

Isolating problems that your product can solve determines your line of questioning.

If you have followed suggestions in the last chapter, you are ready to relate your product's end results to your account's needs. Your line of questioning lets you make points about your product or service and allows the Key Player an opportunity to voice an opinion. Getting people to talk openly about their needs takes careful planning.

I find it helps to learn about the account in three areas. Your first area deals with asking fact-finding questions. The second area combines that objective with the idea of developing the perception of need in your contact's mind. The third area is designed to create urgency to correct the problem or improve the situation and build value for your solution.

Dialogue to get you started:

• Does the account "qualify" for my product?

☎ **"How many employees do you have?"**

☎ **"It would help to know if your company is using a local area network."**

☎ **"Do you ever use outside help for printing manuals?"**

☎ **"How often do you need ...?"**

• Can I isolate an immediate need?

☎ **"Are you looking for new ways to improve your operation?"**

☎ **"I've been reading about your company's success in the international market. How has that affected your shipping costs?"**

☎ **"What do you see as your goal in this area?"**

☎ **"What are your plans for...?"**

☎ **"Are you offering new programs to your clients?"**

☎ **"What are you doing about your banking needs?"**

☎ **"Do you have a back-up plan should something happen?"**

• What would be the value of correcting the account's situation?

☎ **"What do you see as the pluses of this approach?"**

☎ **"Where is this affecting you the most?"**

☎ **"What are the disadvantages of the way you're handling this now?"**

Where to start

When you look at the lead in front of you, do you have enough information to know if this is a potential sale? If the answer is "no, I really don't have enough information," the best use of your time and your account's time is to ask a few straightforward pre-qualifying questions. You described your ideal account in Chapter 3 and prepared Call Strategies in Chapter 4. Use those ideas to help you determine what questions to ask. The answers you receive will signal you to either continue on with the sales process or end the call and move on to the next lead.

TIPSTER

Clarify an
issue as a
problem that
must be solved.

You are beginning the process of finding an "opportunity" for your product so go ahead, probe your contact. The questions should be simple and somewhat broad but very relevant to what you are selling.

Avoid marathon questioning when gathering background information. Limit yourself at the beginning of the call to several well thought out pre-qualifying questions.

We've often been told to ask open-ended questions. Well, I believe your qualifying questions are valuable even if they do elicit a simple answer such as yes or no. The important thing is to learn about the account's immediate situation. For example, if you are selling health insurance to companies with over 25 employees, you might ask, "How many employees do you have?" If the answer is ten, this account doesn't need what you are selling, yet.

Let's say you place temporary employees. You could ask, "Do you ever use outside temporary help?" Or, if you know the account is using a competitor's service, your line of questioning could start with, "When do you need outside temporary help?"

Dialogue to get you started:
- ☎ "How many ...?"
- ☎ "Could you tell me about ...?"
- ☎ "What are you doing about ...?"
- ☎ "What is your situation like today?"
- ☎ "Are you designing new programs?"
- ☎ "Could you tell me about your business? Are you growing?"
- ☎ "What's your annual sales volume?"
- ☎ "When was the last time you spoke to someone about ...?"

Verifying information allows you to draw conclusions about the account's situation. Be sure to get your facts straight so you don't make any wrong assumptions. For example:
- ☎ "I understand there is talk about changing vendors. Do you know if that's true? ... I'd like to be considered."

☎ "I understand you have offices in 30 cities. What plans are you making to add more locations?"

☎ "I've heard you're organizing a new project. Perhaps you can fill me in."

Get the account talking

The way to engage the Key Player in conversation is to ask questions about his needs. The further you question, the more opportunity you provide the contact to tell you what he needs.

Your second line of questioning will isolate problems your product can solve. Find out where and how your product can be used to fix or improve a situation.

Dialogue to get you started:

☎ "What is your opinion of ...?"

☎ "What are your thoughts ...?"

☎ "What are your plans ...?"

☎ "How have you approached the problem of ...?"

☎ "Have you ever heard ...?"

☎ "Is there an immediate need for ...?"

☎ "What are you using now?"

☎ "How do you feel about your current system?"

☎ "What do you like best about the company you're buying from?"

☎ "What are you looking for that you're not getting from your current supplier?"

☎ "Are you talking to anyone else about this issue?"

☎ "Where are most of your advertising dollars spent?"

☎ "What are you spending on office supplies every month?"

☎ "Does your staff ever ask about ...?"

TIPSTER

Stay quiet and give your contact time to think and respond.

Say you are selling a check-writing system and the Key Player tells you he processes 200 checks per month. You may ask, "How much time does that take?" He may at that point say, "Well, it takes too long as far as I'm concerned. We have pretty much outgrown our system." Boom. You now have determined there is a definite need in this account. Resist at this point jumping in and selling the solution. You still don't know many important facts about this account. Summarize his comments. For example, say, "Let me be sure I understand your situation."

After you have a good idea of his needs, you must move intelligently. He may not be making any moves to change his situation. Sure he may be dissatisfied, yet he is at a comfortable level of dissatisfaction. He is not ready to make a move. He doesn't have time. You know all the excuses.

He may wait until he is pressured from external forces (his boss, his budget, his own customers). He may wait until he is completely miserable, To understand this, think about what catalysts are necessary for you personally to begin to change your situation. This is why sales takes more than you saying, "Okay, you need something that I am selling and now you will buy."

TIPSTER

Avoid marathon questioning when gathering background information.

Smart questions move the conversation to a solution

Figure out the strategy to your next line of questioning. Guide calls to areas that have an impact on the account. Say, "What impact does that have on your operation?" Ask questions that create urgency to correct the situation and build value for your solution. Developing the account's urgent nature of his current situation takes time (this may take more than one sales call).

Concentrate on a problem that must be solved. What does the account want most? How can you build sufficient value in his mind to take action now? Your questions will highlight critical situations.

Dialogue to get you started:
- ☎ "Why is that important to you?"
- ☎ "How would that help?"
- ☎ "What would it mean to your bottom line?"
- ☎ "How would it affect your schedule?"
- ☎ "Where is this affecting you the most?"
- ☎ "What impact does it have?"
- ☎ "Will it accommodate the growth you anticipate in the next one to three years?"

☎ "What priorities do you have?"

☎ "Does that have an impact on your production schedule?"

☎ "What would it mean to you to have more time?"

☎ "How would that affect your business? Your profits?"

☎ "Why is that important to you?"

☎ "What is your biggest challenge?"

☎ "What do want to accomplish?"

☎ "Where do most of the problems occur?"

☎ "Are you worried about the quality you get?"

☎ "Does this method give you trouble?"

☎ "If we could improve the quality of this operation, how would that help you?"

Telephone Talk

Listen for ways to develop problems into solutions. Ask questions that help the account visualize improvements. For example, "How would it help you if your staff were more accurate in forecasting their sales?" Or, "How will correcting this affect your situation?"

At this point, it is crucial your contact set up a vision for his department, or entire company. Plan your line of questioning according to responses you anticipate. For example, "What happens when a shipment is late from your supplier? Would it be important for you to solve this problem? How much is it increasing your cost? How would reducing your cost help your operation? Is there any other way this could help you? What other areas are affected the delay."

Get the account to tell you the need is big enough to take action and how much he needs a solution. When the account begins talking "solution" then you reach equal footing, you transform from salesperson selling product, to consultant making recommendations!

TIPSTER

Guide calls to areas that have an impact on the account.

Action Plan

Creative questioning

For each Key Player write a series of questions that pinpoint a specific problem area.

1) Write three questions that help you pre-qualify the account.

2) For each Key Player write three questions that isolate need.

3) Write three questions that help each Key Player understand the value of the solution.

On a final note...

Gathering background information is essential early in the Sales Cycle.

Ask questions which clearly illustrate what the account's situation needs in order to improve, or change.

Get accounts to tell you they need your product, then they will believe in your solution.

Accounts usually make a buying decision when they perceive the problem is larger than the cost of solving it.

TIPSTER

You transform from salesperson to consultant when the account can visualize improvements.

How can I stimulate interest right away?

How will I position my product for the rest
of the conversation?

7

Positioning the Call

Thinking like the account and speaking his language cultivates rapport and acceptance.

Positioning the call means positioning yourself in such a way that when it is time to buy, this account buys from you. People buy products from people. You buy from those people who have built a rapport with you. You accept what they are saying.

We hear a lot about rapport, but what exactly does that mean? I build rapport by thinking like the Key Player—putting myself in his chair on the other end of the phone. To do this, think about what goes through your mind when someone calls you. Probably these three questions:

- How does this call relate to me?
- What does this person want from me?
- How much time is this going to take?

It is up to you to settle those issues and put your contact at ease, immediately. Let's quickly discuss some basic "telephone talk" tips and then go into positioning your call for the most effective sales message.

Can't say it

If you're unable to pronounce the contact's name, don't fake it. Rather than mutilate the name, you can ask for correct pronunciation. Just say, "Hello, I'm calling for Joan .... It looks like I'm going to have a hard time with this last name, can you help me out?"

Name disorder

Somewhere in the history of sales how-to books we were told to say the account's name to personalize the relationship, to get his attention. Now we're all on to that game. When you use someone's name over and over in a conversation, it becomes annoying. Once or twice is okay, otherwise the contact will think you have a name disorder.

And get to the point

Be personable, but not personal. Save the dawdling chatter filled with, "How are you?" for more established relationships. Be someone your contact would like to hear from again.

In the case of referrals, be sure to mention a name when opening the call. "I worked with Amy Hendrickson on a project. Last week she mentioned your name and suggested I get in touch with you."

This is who I am, and this is who I think you are

After you have reached your contact, introduce yourself (avoid the tendency to rush your name). Say who you are, and where you are calling from. If I am calling from out of town, or long distance, I might say that. Sometimes this technique creates a sense of urgency.

To avoid wasting time talking to the wrong person, I always confirm the contact's responsibilities. This helps determine your contact's role and whether he is a Key Player. For example, "I understand you're involved in managing the administrative side of the business. Is that correct?" Or, "I understand you're in the marketing department. Perhaps you can help me. Who makes the decision for selecting printers?"

Telephone Talk

Be conversational

The time you have to grab your contact's attention is narrow. A good way to invite someone to hang up on you is by immediately moving into a monologue or reading directly from a script. For now focus on bringing your contact into the conversation. That means asking a couple of questions and keeping your comments to a minimum.

Dialogue to get you started:

☎ "We're helping other companies improve ...."

☎ "We're new in the area. I wanted to introduce myself and talk to you."

☎ "I stopped by your office the other day. I'm sorry we weren't able to talk. I understand you're very busy."

☎ "I was in your store yesterday. You've done a great job remodeling the interior. What are your plans for the outside? ... I have a couple of ideas that can increase foot traffic."

☎ "There was so much excitement at the conference. I'd like to pick up the conversation where we left off."

☎ "I'm calling to personally invite you to an event we have planned. You may want to attend."

☎ "You may remember us from the conference in Dallas last month. Our company made the keynote address. We talked about the effect of rightsizing in organizations."

☎ "I've heard your name mentioned a few times today."

Can we talk now?

Believe me, you're going to encounter people who are a little bit rough around the edges. A red flag goes up as soon as you hear a gruff voice. My suggestion for working with such people is to be polite and firm. Be sen-

TIPSTER

Be someone
your contact
would like to hear
from again.

sitive that this person may be working under a deadline, may have received some bad news today, had too many calls, or simply may be having an off day.

When I perceive this, I say, "This doesn't sound like a good time for you." Often I will hear my contact sigh in relief, "It really isn't the best day over here." Tune in right away to the contact's mood.

For example:

☎ **"You sound busy. Is there a better time to talk?"**

☎ **"Sounds like you've got a few distractions now, perhaps I should call back at another time. How does your schedule look this afternoon?"**

☎ **"I hear people in your office. If you're in a meeting I can call back."**

You could say, "It's best we talk when we have more time. I have an idea you might want to know about." You can usually find out when your contact has an extra five or ten minutes. You really want his full attention. Set a time to call back. "Perhaps I'll call back this afternoon. Is three o'clock all right with you?"

And then return the call when you said you would. Red-flag cases aside, most people are available to hear your story. I make a habit of asking, "Is this a good time to talk?" People really appreciate asking for permission to use a few moments of their day. One way to grab attention is to put a time limit on the call. "Is this a good time to talk for two minutes?" Accounts usually will carve out 120 seconds from their schedule for you. Make sure you can accomplish an objective in two minutes. Keep your promise. Let your Key Player be the one to spill into overtime.

Don't begin in the middle

Of course, you'll want to tell your Key Players the high points of your product, but not all at once. Have you ever found yourself asking for the order before you really know what would best serve the account? Of course. And how often do you get the order?

When you ask for the order too soon, or pour on too much information too soon, you create the potential to cause resistance or confusion.

Refer to the approach you developed in Chapters 5 and 6 regarding selling solutions and developing need.

If you play it right, you will have plenty of opportunity to present your product and company story. Work on developing rapport and need. There is a logic behind not saying too much too soon. By saying too much early on, you give the account a chance to raise objections.

Stimulate interest right away

Start with the possibility of affecting the buyer's business with a glimpse of the positive end result, so he is willing to continue the conversation. Use a straightforward and helpful approach. A punchy benefit statement is not always the most effective way to start conversations. Think about what goes through your mind when someone makes promises or assumptions about your situation.

Again, jumping into specific solutions before you know the account's situation can open the door for objections.

To cultivate rapport and acceptance, mention your knowledge about what others in the Key Player's industry are doing. Show the account how your experience can help him. Your contact is guaranteed to take notice and listen to what you say next.

Describe your business in simple terms. Explain that you can best serve their needs if you get to know what they do first. For example, "It would help to know what you are doing about ..."

Laying groundwork properly allows you to discuss the most relevant information. Establish that you need information before you can present product or solutions so Key Players are agreeable to your questions.

TIPSTER
Save time.
Confirm each
contact's
responsibilities.

Dialogue to get you started:

☎ **"Hello Karen. This is Bob Kramer with Adler Plus. I'm working with Tom Hunter in Engineering on the upgrade they're designing. I hear you're involved. I'd like to talk over some of our plans with you. Is this a good time?"**

☎ "Hello. My name is Jerry Stone. I understand you're on a committee that's reviewing the way the bank is handling disaster recovery. I'm working with other banks on the same issue. You may be interested in knowing what they're doing. Do you know of our company, Roberston Associates? ... Our expertise is providing disaster recovery solutions for organizations that manage critical and confidential information like banks and hospitals. It would be helpful if I could first learn more about your plans. Do you have about five minutes to talk right now?"

☎ "Good morning, my name is Barbara Winters. I've been told you're the best person to talk to about client billing. There's a possibility we can reduce the number of man hours your lawyers spend tracking this information. You may be interested in hearing how we've streamlined that operation for other law firms in town. We've been working in the legal community for over ten years. You may recall reading about us, The Harper Group, in the Law Journal? ... It would be especially helpful if I could learn about the system you're using. I understand you're very busy. Is this a good time for you to talk for a few minutes?"

More dialogue to get you started:

☎ "Several people at your company have suggested that I talk to you."

☎ "I can tell you what other restaurants are doing."

☎ "No doubt you know of our company, but you may not be aware that we're in the leasing business now."

☎ "I've been thinking about a way we might work together."

☎ "There are some exciting new developments in building security. They could affect your business."

☎ "I have an idea I'd like to talk over with you."

☎ "I hear you're organizing a group to .... I've been working in a similar situation. You may be interested in knowing what we're doing."

Action Plan

Contact connections

1) Review how you acquired each contact's name. Review your approach for Target Markets. (See Chapter 4.) Write an opening statement for each Key Player to stimulate interest right away. Use ideas for your company statement from Chapter 5.

On a final note...

Think like the account.

Your accounts are usually interested in knowing what others in their industry are doing.

Successful salespeople discuss benefits after the call is well in motion. Why? Solutions presented too soon may raise objections.

TIPSTER

Establish the need for more information before asking questions.

When do I leave messages?

How can I take advantage of voicemail?

What do I do if my calls are not returned?

8

Voicemail

Using voicemail effectively can move you forward in the Sales Cycle.

Salespeople have told me they can close business without ever talking to their account in a "live" conversation. They conversed entirely through voicemail. While this might be the exception to the normal way of operating, it illustrates how powerful voicemail can be for accomplishing sales events. Most people in sales today use a combination of voicemail, live conversations, faxes, and E-mail to communicate needs, solutions, negotiations, commitment-to-purchase and so on. The need to develop concise effective communication skills is more and more apparent in today's business world.

The way to develop message-leaving skills is to recognize the messages you respond to. Give heed to those messages left by people you

have never heard from before. Think about your own priorities and response mechanisms. Do you return all calls within a business day? Which messages do you toss, or delete as soon as you receive them? What annoys you about certain messages?

Keep in mind when you leave a voicemail message, you are leaving an imprint of yourself. Beware of sounding distracted, bored, impatient, or disorganized. Your tone should be friendly and professional, your message clear and concise. Practice. Practice. Practice. Also, many voicemail systems allow you to replay your message. Take advantage of this and leave the best message you can. The great thing about voicemail is that your contact can listen to your message more than once. This can definitely work in your favor!

What is the strategy for leaving messages? It is very similar to the methods discussed in Chapter 7 regarding positioning the call. You'll use similar dialogue to create interest, but you'll reorganize the information to suit this one-way mode of conversation.

Some do, others don't

Each industry has its own practice and philosophy about leaving messages be it through voicemail, E-mail or through a message-taker. Some sales colleagues tell me they won't leave messages on a first call to a contact under any circumstance. My position is flexible.

Circumstances vary. I usually test the waters by calling a contact at different times, or researching his schedule before leaving a message. I find correct timing can increase my chances of reaching people directly. For example, "I've been trying to reach Mary Thomas for a couple of weeks now. My timing seems to be off. Perhaps you can fill me in on her schedule. What's the best time of day to reach her?"

If I am still unable to reach the contact, I figure, why go through all the preparation of locating the account, getting a contact name, setting a call objective, just to say, "No, thank you" to an administrative assistant or to hang up on a voicemail box? I prefer to make my time and effort pay off. It often does. After a week of prospecting and leaving messages, I usually receive calls from a handful of people. If you don't leave a message, how is your contact going to call you back? Also, if your contact calls back quickly, that just might be an indication that he is really interested in what you have to say!

How many times?

Basically, for every three to four numbers I dial, I speak to one person on my list. I probably leave messages more than twice as often as I talk to my Key Players. How many times should you call a new contact? Try calling every few days, or weekly. Be wary of pestering the account, hence diluting your effectiveness. Give your contact time to get back to you. He could be very busy, or simply out of town. Often, by the time he responds, you may receive apologies that sound like, "I'm sorry I haven't had a chance to get back to you. I've been buried in deadlines."

Also, managers tell me that if they receive three or four messages from a caller, they'll finally return calls because they feel that maybe you do have something worthwhile to talk about.

Consider varying the times you call. If you are continually missing your contact, perhaps you are hitting his lunchtime, or regularly scheduled meetings. Ask for his direct phone number. Then you can call after 5:00 p.m. or before 8:00 a.m., when many Key Players work at their desks catching up on business outside of traditional work day hours.

TIPSTER

Change your message. Add new ideas. Give reasons for a call back.

Taking advantage of voicemail

Use straightforward information that doesn't reveal too much or over-promise. Why? You don't want to give Key Players reasons to shoot down your idea or form a defense perimeter before you talk to them.

Review the way you are beginning your conversations in Chapter 7, and adopt those ideas for your voicemail message. The strategy for invoking a response is very similar to the way you encourage a live conversation to continue.

One technique I use to be sure the contact knows how the call relates to him is to ask, "What's in it for the contact to return my call?" Put your answer in the message. Your contact will listen to voicemail all the way through and likely find a reason for talking to you.

Dialogue to get you started:

☎ "Hello Karen. This is Bob Kramer with Adler Plus. I'm working with Tom Hunter in Engineering on the upgrade they're designing. I hear you're involved. I'd like to talk over some of our plans with you. I'm meeting with Tom next Tuesday morning. Perhaps, we could set aside time to meet at 11 o'clock for about 15 minutes if your schedule is free. My number is 555-9852. If I'm not there, you can leave a message on my voicemail. If you're available, I'll put you on my schedule. Take care."

TIPSTER

Help screeners
sell benefits
of your product
to Key Players.

☎ "Hello. This is Jerry Stone with Roberston Associates. We're in the business of providing disaster recovery solutions for organizations that manage critical and confidential information. I understand you're on a committee that's reviewing the way the bank is doing this. I'd like to talk to you when you have about five minutes. I'm working with other banks on the same issue. You may be interested in hearing what they're doing. You can reach me at 555-4378. I'm usually in my office until six o'clock every day. Again, my number is ...."

☎ "Good morning, my name is Barbara Winters with The Harper Group. You may have noticed mention of us in the Law Journal. We've been working in the legal community for over ten years. I've been told you're the best person to talk to about client billing. We have a program that can reduce the number of man hours lawyers spend tracking this information. We're working with other law firms in town. You may be interested in hearing what results they're getting. I'm out of the office for the rest of the week but I do want to talk with you. I'll call on Monday. I understand the best time for you is after five o'clock, so I'll try back then."

☎ "I have an idea I'd like to talk over with you. It's about ...."

☎ "I've tried reaching you directly, but my timing is off. I hope we can talk soon."

☎ "It's about the planning department approving your projects."

☎ "You can reach me after 4 P.M."

☎ "I was hoping we could talk today. Sorry I missed you."

☎ "My name is .... I know we've never talked although I have tried to reach you several times. It's probably best to leave a message now. Hope to talk soon."

Introduce who you are. Focus first on your company, and then move into how you think your contact may be involved in the problem/solution.

Mention referrals.

Speak clearly in a conversational tone. Don't rush your name or message. Avoid slowing down to a crawl. Spell your name if necessary. This will also help your contact to pronounce your name on the call back.

Most important, suggest a time you can be reached.

And repeat your telephone number.

A new spin on return calls

Use the option on voicemail to locate other people who have knowledge of the buyer's schedule and can offer information about the situation. Change your message by adding new ideas, including new reasons for a call back. Send an E-mail message. Show you're serious and confident about the possibility of working together. For example:

☎ "This is ... again. I don't want to be bothersome but other people at your company have told me you're looking for ways to improve .... There's a possibility we can help. I understand you start your day early. I do, too. I know you're very busy. Perhaps we can talk one morning while it's quiet. My direct number is ...."

☎ "I've talked to several people in your organization. I understand you're the best person to start with about public relations."

Message-takers have info

Message-takers are often screening out unwanted calls. You know the drill. Be prepared for the question, "What's this in reference to?" So, address issues that pass the screening test. The clearer you are about a situation the easier it is for screeners to encourage Key Players to take action.

Dialogue to get you started:

☎ "... I understand he's reviewing the way the bank is planning for disaster recovery. That's what we do. He may be interested in hearing what plans other banks are making. I only need about five minutes of his time to get started. What is the best time of the day to reach him? ... I wouldn't know what information to send until we talk more. How does his schedule look for this week?"

☎ "... I've been told she's the best person to start with about client billing. We have a program that can reduce the amount time lawyers spend tracking this information. She may be interested in hearing what other law firms in town are doing. ... Yes, there is a possibility he knows us from the <u>Law Journal</u>."

I recruit each administrative assistant, receptionist and work group colleague to be a part of my quest. Sort of the minor league players in the Sales Cycle. After my introduction, I briefly explain my objective, and ask a few questions. For example, I may inquire about the schedule of my hard-to-reach contact, or other Key Players involved.

Always keep in mind that message-takers have access to different types of information. If you are continually leaving messages with an administrative assistant, for example, you might say, "I've been trying to reach him for a few days now, is he out of town?" If so, use the opportunity to get names of other Key Players involved in the Buying Process. Say, "Is there someone else who can help me?" Or, "Who does he work with regarding those issues?"

Dialogue to get you started:

☎ "I start my day early. Are mornings a good time for reaching him? ... How early is he in the office?"

☎ "I've been told he is the best person to start with about employee benefits."

☎ "I understand she approves the sales budget. Is that true? ... What groups report to her? What is her title?"

☎ "I'm calling about a meeting next Thursday morning for controllers and other financial people. Do you know if his calendar is free? ... Oh, I see. Perhaps there's someone he would trust who I should talk to about this. Where do you suggest I start?"

☎ "I understand there is talk about changing vendors. Do you know if that's true?"

☎ "Does he use voicemail? Is there a way for you to put me through?"

☎ "Is there a way to go directly to voicemail and leave a message for him?"

☎ "What on-line service does he use? Can you tell me his E-mail address?"

Message-takers are people, too. Show your appreciation. For example, say, "I appreciate your help. By the way, I didn't get your name."

Create a sense of urgency

Sometimes you need to speak to a Key Player in a hurry. Once I had a contract nearly complete, but I needed paperwork from purchasing. My company had already guaranteed delivery. I introduced myself to my Key Player's colleague and described my dilemma.

"Perhaps you can help. There may be someone in purchasing I can talk with. I understand you can help. We have a deadline I hope we can meet. Any suggestions?"

When my job is to close the sale, I aim to keep the ball in my court. Rarely will I ever sit back and wait for results.

Practice professional courtesies

If you left a message for one contact, and another person resolved your problem or answered your question, call your first contact back. Let him know your concerns have been addressed.

Also, avoid leaving a message unless you can be reached. State a window of time you will be available.

Be prepared for a call back!

Consider this scenario. Your contact is not in. You leave a powerful message. You move on to the next two hours of cold calls. After lunch your phone rings and it's an unfamiliar voice with a vaguely familiar name attached. He says he is returning your call. Aaargh. You can't remember why you called or who this person is! "Where are my notes? A call back I wasn't expecting!" you say to yourself. Hopefully you've been taking good notes during your prospecting. But how do your recover from this faux pas?

Here is a great way to buy some time. "It's great to hear from you. Can you hold for a moment, while I change phones? I'm not at my desk." Collect your notes and your thoughts and go to it. And congratulations, you've just succeeded in leaving an effective message.

TIPSTER

Get your contact's direct number. Try calling outside traditional hours.

Action Plan

Get the message?
1) Prepare a voicemail message for each Key Player.

2) Write an "opening statement" you can use with people who screen your calls or take messages for your Key Players. Screeners will usually ask, "What is this in reference to?" Write possible responses.
Hint: You now have an opportunity to ask fact-finding questions that will help you understand more about the account's situation.

On a final note...

Transmitting enthusiasm through word choice and voice inflection shows you have conviction, which encourages people to take action.

Key Players who appear to be ignoring your messages are often legitimately busy. They will often get back to you after three or more calls.

Message-takers can usually answer some of your questions and put you in touch with other Key Players, so ask for their help and advice.

How can I prevent objections?

How do I handle objections?

9

Preventing and Handling Objections

Concentrating on customer needs dissolves many objections.

Your top leads are valuable. They cost too much time to find and cultivate for you to fail because you didn't plan a tight presentation, i.e., learn how to deal with objections. And yet many salespeople flinch upon hearing the slightest inflection of "no, thank you. I'm not interested."

How does your account know he's not interested? Does he know what he needs? Do you know what he needs? Has he heard your solution?

One of the hardest elements of making new business contacts (and the whole sales process) is sorting through objections. How do you decide if what you're hearing is a valid objection, or a case of the "brush off?"

TIPSTER

The best
way to deal with
objections
is prevention.

Objections are stumbling blocks for many of us, and the best way to deal with them is prevention. My advice is to go back and follow my previous advice. Using the Power Calling approach outlined to this point will help you prevent objections.

As salespeople, we often create a situation where our Key Player brings in the objection. We actually invite the roadblock!

This is an issue of timing your information during the presentation. Look at how much information you are revealing. Pay attention to when objections come up. Rather than ask why your accounts say "no," listen to when your accounts say "no." For example, if you notice an objection happens very early in the call, or the Sales Cycle, more often than not, your contact is objecting to your approach, not your product.

In other words, you may be jumping in too fast, selling your product before you understand the problems.

The answer is to avoid talking about solutions until you and the account have discussed, established, and agreed upon a real need. At that point, you are on the same path, and you can move forward with the appropriate benefit statements. Thus preventing "false" objections.

Sometimes it's true

Like it or not, sometimes objections are valid. It is up to you to recognize the signs.

Make an honest judgement call on whether or not you can improve the account's current situation. Or, if you can coexist with a current supplier or competitor. If not, your account will appreciate your next move. Simply say, "Perhaps there isn't a need right now, would you mind if I phoned you in three months? And please keep my card in your file in case your situation should change."

Otherwise, as you begin to use the Power Calling approach you will encounter objections you must prepare for. Now is when we call in "The Big Three."

Three steps to handling an objection.

• Acknowledge the account's position. Be genuine. This is about putting yourself in your Key Player's shoes. Let him know you are on his side, that you are looking for a solution not a sale. Consider this a challenging opportunity to build rapport.

Dialogue to get you started:
☎ "I see your point of view."
☎ "I can understand how you could feel that way."
☎ "I understand your concern."
☎ "I've heard that concern before."

• Summarize the objection. Ask questions and be sure the answers are clear to you. Be attentive. This step is very important. You must be sure you are addressing the concern accurately. Also, you want to whittle away objections that may not be valid. Don't assume you understand why your account is saying no. Keep communication open and the rapport will continue to grow. This is also your opportunity to let your account know you hear him. What does this do? It builds trust, a key to sales.

Dialogue to get you started:
☎ "What I hear you saying ...."
☎ "I think I understand. Are you saying that ...?"
☎ "I'm not sure I understand. Are you saying that ...?"
☎ "Sounds like you may have had a bad experience. What happened?"
☎ "There must be a very good reason you're saying that. It would help to know more."
☎ "It would help if we could talk a little bit more about ...."
☎ "Are you saying that you're concerned ...? When is the last time you looked at other options?"

TIPSTER
Objections heard
early in the call
may refer to your
approach, not
your product.

• Make a decision. Ask yourself, "Is this a mismatch or is there something more I need to know about this account?" To determine if an objection is valid, probe for more information. Isolate problem areas using a line of questioning from ideas found in Chapter 6.

Dialogue to get you started:

☎ "I don't think I know enough about your situation. It would be especially helpful if you could tell me about ...."

☎ "How are you handling ...?"

☎ "How do you feel about your current system?"

☎ "What do you like best about doing business with your current supplier?"

☎ "What are you looking for that you're not getting from them?"

☎ "What are you doing about ...?"

☎ "And, you're wondering what I'm going to tell you that makes my company different. I don't think I know enough about your company to answer that."

I'm happy with my current supplier

One very common objection you'll hear is that your account is happy with the person with whom is currently doing business. This "business as usual" or "thanks, but no thanks" response to your offering means your account is unwilling to take a risk of changing, or is unwilling to make the effort and test the waters. It's up to you to change his mind on this "status quo" approach to doing business. Do you have "new" options for him to consider? Will he listen to what you have to offer?

Consider this: if your account is happy with his current supplier, that means he has a need for your product or service. You could then label this an encouraging and positive objection.

Here is another approach to try. Set up the scenario of problem-solution. You described problems and your solution for each Target Market in Chapter 4. Use that information to help you build a list of likely problems, betting the account has experienced a few of them.

Let's say you place temporary employees. Start with the most likely issues. For example, "Other buyers in your position have told me that temps often don't show up for assignments, or will drop out of an eight assignment after two weeks. They're also saying .... Have any of these things ever happened to you?" Say your contact responds, "Well, yes, actually that does happen. What makes you different?" This establishes an opportunity for you to discuss the specific end results of your product or service.

On the other hand, after you have set up the scenario and the account is not experiencing any of those detailed difficulties, he may not be a good candidate. Offer to be available if something should change and move onto your next lead.

Using the objection to your advantage

Once I spoke with a decision maker who played the "We're going to put the decision off" tune. My position was let's do business, now.

"I don't think we should make any changes for at least 60 days," he said. "There's a risk the installation will interrupt production and cause a delay in our schedule. We can't afford that."

These are delicate twists that come up in sales. The next thing I would say would be crucial to moving the sale to a close—this month. If we waited, there may not be a close in 60 days, or 60 months. "That's precisely the reason we should go ahead. And as quickly as possible," I said. "I spoke to your colleague Jim Elliott last week about this very issue. He believes he can cut production time by 30 percent or more if we go ahead now. We've also worked out an installation schedule. It should go something like this ...."

TIPSTER

Make a judgement call. Can you truly improve the account's situation?

This technique of providing details to actually substantiate his objection moves things out of the rut. Try using the Key Player's own objection to show him exactly how your product will benefit him if he moves now. Allow yourself to use the data you've gathered to push past any resistance.

Beware of blockers

So far we have discussed those sticky situations called objections that your Key Players throw at you. But what about the frustrating gatekeepers that can stop you from even getting your foot in the door?

say, "I wasn't aware you made those types of decisions for the company. How do you fit in over there? I didn't mean to overlook anyone. Maybe we should meet." Say this in light spirit and you'll probably get some movement in your sales call.

I often take a blocker by the hand and lead him down my path of reason. For example, if I am trying to gather names, my strategy is to ask how decisions are made and about the people who are affected.

Dialogue to get you started:

☎ "Do you make decisions alone?"

☎ "Who do you rely on for advice about ...?"

☎ "How is ... planned?"

☎ "How is it approved?"

☎ "What groups are affected by this?"

☎ "We might gather some good ideas if we invite people from that department. They are usually quite helpful with their questions and concerns?"

☎ "Another client of mine waited until too long before talking to end-users. That was quite a setback. Maybe we should get them in-volved right away."

Action Plan

Roadblock removal

1) What two common objections you most often hear?

2) Address each objection using techniques learned in this chapter.

On a final note...

Successful salespeople receive fewer objections because they have mastered the art of prevention.

Notice where the objection occurs in the conversation. Objections raised early in the call suggests that you offered too much information too soon.

An objection may indeed signify a mismatch. Accounts may not have a need for your product. Or perhaps the competition has a clear advantage.

Have I successfully addressed the buyer's key concerns?

What commitment is needed to make the call a success?

10

Commitment

Agreeing on a specific action moves the sale closer to a buying decision.

When your conversation is flowing, closing the call will happen naturally. Take the lead. It is best to end the call by proposing an action that will move you to the next step in the Sales Cycle. Closing the call on a positive note is a great success, but obtaining commitment from your account is what you really need.

Set a realistic goal. If you have followed the Power Calling approach, your closing goal is synonymous with your call objective. (Refer to Chapter 4 to refresh your memory.) During the conversation look for opportunities where you can begin your close and design your commitment actions. Agree on the logical next step. Get your account committed.

Involve your Key Player. Decide on an action he will take, be it talking with his colleagues, scheduling a meeting, agreeing to read your product literature. By involving your account, you are making him responsible for his word. His reputation as a professional is now tested. He has now invested some time in the phone call, promises to act between calls, and to talk to you again soon.

Be ready with several alternatives. By giving your Key Player a choice of actions and commitments, he may feel more in control. We all appreciate options.

Dead air closing in

When is it time to go for the commitment? Be aware of telephone talk dynamics. Ever feel the conversation dulling, losing its edge? Your Key Player sighs, and then you squirm through extended silence. You know the interaction is headed in a positive direction, but is breaking down. That's a major clue to pull the conversation together and close the call.

For example:

☎ "I have a suggestion."

☎ "I have a couple of ideas."

☎ "From what you're saying, it seems we could show you ...."

☎ "It occurs to me there's a way for us to work together ...."

☎ "It occurs to me you would want to know a little more about what we do ...."

☎ "Perhaps we can get to know each other by starting ...."

☎ "It helps me to meet people in person."

☎ "Maybe we can get to know each other a little better by exchanging some information."

☎ "Let's get together and talk more."

This is not to say that you wait for the dead air to close in. Instinct will tell you when it's closing time.

The Power Caller takes these steps:

• Ask yourself, "Have I successfully addressed the buyer's key concerns?" Take the initiative. Summarize the call with important points. Ask the account if you've overlooked anything. Use ideas for presenting your company and product from Chapter 5, Selling Solutions, Problem Solving.

For example:

☎ **"And another way this will help you is the way you can compile programs. You'll be able shorten development time. That can take some pressure off the overtime problem, and you can still meet your deadline. I think that covers everything. But before we go any further, have I overlooked any areas you'd like to know more about? ... Then let me cover that now. The way it works is .... Is there any other way this could be useful?"**

• Ask yourself, "What commitment is needed to make the call a success?" Propose a specific action that the Key Player is likely to accept. If there is resistance, be prepared with an alternate suggestion so the Key Player doesn't stall the buying decision.

TIPSTER

Propose a specific action that your contact is likely to accept.

Dialogue to get you started:

☎ **"It's easy to get started. I'll take care of the details. All I need from you is ...."**

☎ **"I have a couple of ideas for you. I'll fax them right away. How does your schedule look this afternoon? ... Let's review the information together later today while it's still fresh in our minds."**

☎ **"I'd like to show you our work. It probably won't take more than 15 minutes. I'm in your area most of next week. Is your calendar handy?"**

☎ **"How would you go about discussing this with your staff? ... Should a member of your staff sit in on the meeting?"**

☎ "Projects like yours usually take three months or more to work out all the details. I would propose you get started right away if you plan to be ready by June. I have a suggestion, let's meet next week. How do you feel about that?"

☎ "I'll get samples out to you right away. Let's schedule time next week to talk again. I'd like to personally review the information with you."

☎ "If you're more comfortable, we could start with a ...."

☎ "If you like what you see, are you going to have anyone else review this?"

☎ "I'd like to show you our work. I think you'll be impressed with the way we handle imaging."

Do we understand each other?

At this point you move in to accomplish the goal of the call or series of calls. You send the literature, you make the appointment, you send the product out for evaluation, examination, or analysis, whatever your sales event may be. Now is the time to make arrangements to complete this stage of the sale with this particular Key Player. Set the stage for follow up calls. Now is the time for hand holding.

TIPSTER

Give the contact a way to reach you before you get off the phone.

Be specific about what you are going to do next. And communicate that action clearly.

Be specific about what you expect from this Key Player.

Be specific about the time and content of the next sales call. I cannot stress this enough. You must make your account do homework while you are not working with him directly. Earlier, we discussed how a lot of selling goes on behind the scenes. This is where it happens.

For example, remind the Key Player you will speak to his colleague and hope he will do the same. Remind the Key Player to invite other Key Players to the meeting you have set up. When you send literature, highlight specific lines in the brochure. Make a note, for example, saying. "Take a close look at pages three and seven. You may want to discuss the information on page four with your staff."

Dialogue to get you started:

☎ "I'll call everyone else right away. I know that you're very busy."

☎ "That's going in the mail today. Let's schedule time to talk again next week."

☎ "I have a couple of ideas but I'd like to do a little homework first and get back to you."

☎ "Will you personally review the material? ... It should only take about 15-20 minutes. How much time do you need before we talk again?"

☎ "It should only take about ten minutes to review. When do you think you can get to this?"

☎ "When do you expect to know the names of everyone attending the workshop?"

TIPSTER

Closing the call
on a positive
note is great,
but commitment
is what you're
aiming for.

When you work this way, your next call is always more effective at moving the account forward. This method allows the account to make best use of his time. It makes him an active member of the sales process and Sales Cycle, rather than a barrel gathering features and benefits from a salesperson.

Your first call to a contact is the time kick off a new business relationship.

Avoid the know-it-all syndrome

Telephone Talk

Pretending you know something, when you don't just won't work in cold calling. Don't be afraid to say, "I am not sure. But I'll be happy to research that for you and call you back."

I relish the times when a Key Player asks a question I cannot answer. It is my chance to be a consultant, to be helpful. We cannot always address every issue that arises, so we call on our resources. If an account expresses serious interest in your product, you may call in your technical support department, for example, or your sales manager. Your approach may go like this:

Telephone
Talk

"That's a good question. I've made a note to get an answer for you. It also occurs to me that we have something you'd like to know a lot more about. I'd like you to talk to our specialist. Let's set aside time for all of us to meet in person. I'll E-mail some information to you so you may review it before the meeting."

At times—when you don't want your Key Player to know everything you know—it's okay to be vague about details. Sometimes you may not want to answer all the questions. This is a way for you to stay in touch, to keep the dialogue open and moving forward.

Sounds obvious, but...

Amid the enthusiasm from an unexpected quick and positive response we receive from a Key Player, we agree to a plan, then hang up—and then whack ourselves in the head.

Have you ever ended a conversation and realized that your wonderful contact has no way to reach you? Does he know your name, and who your company is? Always remember to give the person a way to get a hold of you, just in case he has any questions or concerns. Be sure to repeat and spell your name. And give him your telephone and fax number, and E-mail address. Say, "Before we go, do you have a piece of paper and a pencil handy? Again, my name is ...."

Now that you're off the phone

Being a professional is knowing that what you do is important, and that you recognize that doing it to the best of your ability is essential. People who take care about their work and take pride in their work strive for total quality. You are reliable. Fulfill your promises.

When you hang up the phone execute the plan you and your account agreed upon. Take care of all the details on your end. Put your plan in motion and work out the next call objective and the commitment associated with it.

Action Plan

Get the account moving
1) Write a specific action your account is likely to accept.

2) Write an alternative action. Refer to sales events and call objectives in Chapter 2—The Sales Cycle, Selling Events.

On a final note...

Obtaining commitment is a natural conclusion to a properly handled call.

You may have to change your call objective midstream, so it's helpful to plan alternate actions.

After the account agrees to take action, you have accomplished your goal. It's time to get off the phone.

TIPSTER
Leave the
account
feeling good
about hearing
from you again.

What have I learned that will influence
future calls on this account?

What have I learned that I can integrate
into my overall sales technique?

11

Follow-up

Turning details into useful information and analyzing your effectiveness after every call improves selling technique.

Every time you speak to a Key Player, you're building an account history. This means you are the appointed historian. So keep accurate records. On a basic level, your accounts will see you are "on the ball," that you know what is going on. In a pinch, you never know when your recorded details will come in handy. There will come a day when your impeccable note-taking will lure in that sale that almost got away.

Summarize your notes after every call. Get the conversation out of your head and committed to paper or database.

Ironically, if you operate from memory alone, your accounts will not be impressed with your memory. Conversely, when you keep accurate details in accessible files—again, on paper or in a database—then your contacts will be amazed with your memory!

TIPSTER

Every time you speak to a Key Player, you're building an account history.

Not only will they be impressed, they will believe you are concerned with their situation. Your knowledge and recollection of details will "comfort" your accounts. They want to know they are in good hands, that you are "taking care" of them. Remember, people buy from people. This grand effect is the result of simple organization on your part. Below is the drill you should follow to improve your position within accounts. Do this when you get off the phone or return from your meeting.

How do I feel about the sales call?

Did I meet my call objective?

Did I need to alter my call objective midway through?

Did I plan for an alternate objective?

Did I meet that objective?

What promises did I make?

What is the next step with this buyer?

When do I follow up?

Which areas did the buyer feel strongly about and why?

Which specific questions had the most influence, effects, or results?

What did I learn about the account's Buying Process?

What did I learn about Key Players?

What did learn that I can use on future calls into the account?

Reaching the moment of truth

Here is a scenario of the salesperson who keeps records in his memory. The phone rings into the salesperson's office.

"Hi, this is Bill Bates," says the caller.

The salesperson responds with silence, thinking, this name sounds familiar. But he keeps sketchy notes in a disorganized fashion. He finds a piece of paper that reads Bill Bates, nothing more. "Oh, hello Bill," he fumbles. "How can I help you?" Bill needs to remind why he is calling—the salesperson called him months ago and now he is ready to buy. Except now Bill Bates is not too impressed with the salesperson's lack of knowledgeable response.

Let's rewind the video and push play. We can re-establish rapport immediately with an old account. Here's how.

An incoming caller announces he is Bill Bates.

"Bill, good to hear from you," says the salesperson. "May I put you on hold while I change phones?" He flips to the "B" section in his database and find Bates, Bill. That's right. He's the guy who was expanding his franchises and wouldn't be ready for our software system until the fall. At the time you thought he was giving you the "we're putting the decision off indefinitely" tune. You were rather skeptical of this sale ever closing. Nevertheless, the notes mention a follow-up date for October. It's September. Bill is on the ball and so are you.

"Thanks for holding, Bill. Your expansion must be moving right along. Are you on schedule? Tell me about your plans for your inventory system." Bill is now at ease, and the relationship picks up on a positive note and moves forward.

Golden Selling Hours

TIPSTER

Implementing a lot of changes overnight is not the wisest approach.

Now that you are organized and take copious notes after every call, it is time to evaluate your effectiveness.

Devise a time-management schedule and stick to it. Again, devote certain hours to prospecting only. This also applies to your Target Markets. When you call those accounts in the same Target Markets in the same time block you'll feel the momentum growing from call to call.

Keep Key Player's work habits in your notes. Always ask "when is a good time to reach you?" If you haven't asked for his direct number yet, do. Remember, many executives either work late or arrive at the office early. You are very likely to bypass receptionists during these hours. Note the time and dates of all your calls.

Keep track of your progress. How many calls are you making every day? How much time do you spend telephone prospecting? How long is each call? If your situation is like most sales, you are probably paid according to results, not hours spent, or wasted. Strive to work smart, not work more. Notice the time of day when your energy level is highest. Are your calls more successful then? If so, those may be your golden selling hours.

Count the calls you make each day. How many stories did you tell? Keep a list of successful calls and not-so-successful calls. Keeping records on yourself can be a brutally honest experience at first, and if you don't like what you are seeing the only place to go is up! By each week's end, you can congratulate yourself, or kick yourself, gently.

Improving your skills

If you are looking to improve your sales techniques, which in turn should lift your "numbers," changes must be made. However, implementing a lot of changes overnight is not the wisest thing to do. I suggest pinpointing a few areas where there is room for improvement. Make a list of specifics that you have control over. For example, you probably don't have control over product improvement. You do however, have control over your time, your dialogue, your schedule, etc. Be realistic and you'll have greater success when making changes to your workday.

In order to measure your results, choose one variable at a time, try it for a specified time—for a week, or month—and then compare.

What one change would *really* improve my results?

More preparation
More time
More/better contacts
More/better leads
Changes to dialogue
More/better appointments
Better qualified accounts
Shorter Sales Cycle
Less talking/more listening
Improved product knowledge
Fewer objections
Better understanding of the competition
More return calls/less voicemail
Better follow through

Relax and try some humor

Add a spirited quality to your words. Laughter is a universal experience. It's a great ice-breaker. I like to sprinkle wit and humor into the conversation as long as it rings true to the sales call. If I find humor in a situation, I don't wait self-consciously for my contact to laugh, I laugh first. Enthusiasm is contagious.

One of the most difficult elements of selling by phone is allowing your best self to shine through the telephone line. How easy it is to slip into a monotone voice after a few hours of prospecting. One way to stay fresh is to view each call as though it is the first of the day. Believe that with this call, you'll make a move toward a sale. If that call is a dud, then you are one call closer to finding your ideal account!

Action Plan

The road to your success
Improving your selling technique involves getting honest with yourself. Ask these questions and commit your answers to paper.
1) What have I learned that I can improve on future calls into this account?

2) What have I learned that I can use in other selling situations?

3) What have I learned that I can use for this Target Market?

On a final note...

Successful salespeople know how to use detail to their advantage. They understand the importance of getting the detail right.

If you want to keep getting what you're getting, keep doing what you're doing. If you don't want what you are getting, it's time to make a change.

If you're working on improving your sales technique, change one variable at a time and watch the results.

TIPSTER
Your flawless
note-taking
will someday lure
in that sale
that almost
got away.

How do I feel about the progress I'm making?

What specific actions will improve my position?

12

Follow-Through Strategies

Testing your progress with accounts determines future Selling Events.

Test your progress with accounts by comparing what you're doing now, versus what you would like to be doing. Find gray areas that need your attention. Mysteries are often solved by asking questions. This calls for you to refer to your account's Sales Cycle and Buying Process. Have you skipped over some Selling Events? What specific objectives have you yet to meet?

Check notes before a Selling Event begins so you're certain of the call objective. If you find some internal dialogue in your head going back and forth about an issue with an account, don't leave suspicions in your head. Take care of them. Confirm everything. Remember in the be-

ginning of the book we talked about how, mysteriously, we sometimes lose a sale? This is when it occurs—when you have an unsettled feeling that "something is up" with the account and you don't follow your instinct. Don't ignore those feelings. Get to the bottom of it.

Devise a plan to contact people regularly. As time passes, enthusiasm for your product presentation dwindles, and that can stall a buying decision if you're not actively involved. Develop one strong ally in the account. He may provide help and advice. He can sell on your behalf behind the scenes.

Look for missing information, organizational changes, uncontacted players and other developments that might slow down the buying decision. By keeping in touch with Key Players in an account, you keep abreast of changing needs, staff changes, and new monkey wrenches in the Buying Process.

Decide a specific action you can take to keep the sale moving forward toward the close.

Where did I go wrong?

Analyze your "lost" sales, and you'll discover ways to improve future Selling Events with current accounts. Common threads are woven through lost sales. If you find them, you can fix them. Only by taking a serious look at those accounts can you gain insight. An evaluation will highlight areas for you to focus on. Look for patterns that repeat themselves. Below are some questions to ask yourself.

How did I lose the sale?

Where in the Sales Cycle did I discover the sale was lost?

What were the warning signs?

Did I identify everyone in the Buying Group, know their roles, and understand how they influenced each other?

Did I have credibility with the Buying Group?

What did each Key Player think about my proposal?

Did I have at least one person I consulted for information? Did I have a Key Player who guided me with other Key Players and who was selling on my behalf behind the scene?

Was each Key Player able to explain or describe the benefits to other Key Players?

Did I understand the Key Player's needs?

How well did our product meet the account's needs?

What results did I stress?

Was each Key Player confident and enthusiastic about our solution?

Did someone sabotage the order?

Did I screen out the competition and current supplier?

Did each Key Player know our strengths?

What was each Key Player's concerns?

Did I have credibility with the decision maker?

Use this to plan specific actions you would take if you were starting over again.

Improving your position

When you sit down to review your forecast of sales, be honest with yourself. Are you making progress? Do you really know where you stand within your accounts? Have buying decisions slipped? Have buying decisions stalled? Do you have accounts that feel "uncomfortable?" Look for red-flag situations that require you to take action right away.

Conversely, be wary of "the sure thing." I suggest you put a red flag next to sales you have "in the bag." Overconfidence may signal an oversight on your part. As we have said, no one likes to be surprised with a sudden "no sale" ringing on the register. It happens, but doesn't always have to. Here's how to get a handle on them.

Give "tough" accounts formal evaluations. Trouble areas will be highlighted. Fill in the blanks to the following questions:

Am I making progress?

What am I doing with the account now?

What would I like to be doing?

What question does the Key Player want answered?

Have I identified everyone in the Buying Group, defined their roles, and do I understand how they influence each other?

TIPSTER

Analyze lost sales and discover ways to improve your sales technique.

How well does our product meet their needs?

What results should I be stressing?

Do I have credibility with the Buying Group?

What does each Key Player think about my proposal?

Do I have at least one person I can go to for advice or information that can guide me with other people and who can sell on my behalf?

How well can each Key Player explain or describe the benefits to other Key Players?

Do I have credibility with the decision maker?

What's in it for them?

Who might sabotage the order?

Have I screened out the competition and current supplier?

What does each Key Player see as our strengths and weaknesses? What is my response?

How confident and enthusiastic is each Key Player about my product?

Where do we go from here?

Dialogue to get you started:

☎ "I would really appreciate your advice."

☎ "Something has come up that you may want to know about."

☎ "I realized that we've never really talked ...."

☎ "It occurred to me we should take a look at a couple of issues that I may have overlooked."

☎ "How do you feel about the progress we're making?"

☎ "Is there anything standing in the way of our doing business together?"

☎ "Have we covered all the important issues?"

☎ "I understand there are some new developments."

☎ "I've heard about the reorganization. How does this affect our doing business?"

☎ "What concerns do you have?"

☎ "What have you heard about ...?"

☎ "You might like to know about the progress I'm making. We haven't talked in a while. What progress are you making? I noticed in my calendar that you're planning to install the evaluation today. How's that going?"

☎ "It's been a week since you turned the proposal over to the committee. What have you heard?"

☎ "We were planning to talk today. Is this a good time?"

☎ "Are we on schedule?"

☎ "Do you have any concerns about the budget?"

Sales don't stop there

Follow-through also applies to the successful sales. Soothe and congratulate your new clients and customers on making a good decision. They may suffer what is called "buyer's uncertainty." We've all had that experience. After we bought and paid for something, we look for ways to justify the purchase. Help your clients overcome their uncertainties once the sale is concluded. Send a new customer a letter saying you are pleased about the new business relationship. You look forward to serving the account now and in the future.

Professionals work hard to build and maintain unique business relationships. Closing the big sale, moving on and never contacting the buyer again is not a recipe for rapport.

No news is not good news

Customer service and satisfaction is becoming more and more important these days. People want value for their money. I think you'll agree from a consumer's point of view that it is bad form for a salesperson to disappear after product and money are exchanged.

TIPSTER

Filter out who or what is slowing down the buying decision.

As a salesperson, be sure the sale is complete even after you have commission in pocket. Be there when things go wrong. Express your regrets for the situation and be genuinely concerned about finding a solution. After you and your account agree upon a solution, take action immediately. Be the liaison with your customer service department if need be.

Remain open and honest with your customers and clients. When you are, even when news is not so great, a funny thing happens—the client remains loyal. And a loyal customer is a repeat customer, and that makes your job easier and more rewarding!

Do your best

When you notice you're making too many calls with too few results, look for concrete actions you can take to boost your numbers. First thing you should do is tell yourself that your job is important, that you are working to make improvements—significant, be they large or small—in people's work situations.

Next, ask yourself, "Am I doing the best I can do? Where is there room for improvement?" You may find an area that you can alter just a bit. Watch what happens when you do. More often than not, new life will be breathed into your sales technique.

As with most things in life, it's important for you to periodically review your performance. Power Calling is no exception.

TIPSTER
Give "tough" accounts formal evaluations. Trouble areas will be highlighted.

On a final note...

Locate areas of weakness that can jeopardize the sale. Study your options.

The important element of following-through is to know where you are now and where you have to go to close the sale.

Analyzing lost accounts improves future Selling Events.

TIPSTER
Listen to
gut feelings.
Most have merit.

Order more Power Calling products and programs

Ask about action planners, training programs, and workshops. We welcome distributors for our products and programs. Call us or write.

Power Calling
P.O. Box 497
Calistoga, CA 94515
TEL: (707) 942-5291
FAX: (707) 942-4583